"Tom, have [illegible]
or not?" Sydn[illegible]

At last she [illegible]
pacing and looked at her.

"Well?" she asked, hands on her hips. "I'm waiting. Are we in love or not?"

He frowned. A glimmer of his spirit shone in his eyes, and his lips began to form a lopsided grin. "Why do you ask?"

"Because I want to know. Because I've been dreaming about falling in love since I was a little girl, and I have certain expectations and conditions I want met."

His brows rose with amusement and interest. "Like what?"

"Well," she said, "I expect it to be a sharing thing. Rich and poor. Good and bad. I don't expect to be happy all the time. I expect the person I fall in love with to share my troubles with me. And I expect to share his."

He wasn't laughing anymore. He was in love. She didn't know what she was asking for, but he liked the way she was thinking. If she hadn't looked so serious, he'd have grabbed her and kissed her until she went limp in his arms—and even then he wouldn't have let go of her. "What if this other person's problem could destroy the love between you? Would you still want to hear it?"

"Would it be something so horrible it couldn't be forgiven?" she asked.

"No, more like something that would have to be lived with. Always there, out in the open." He looked at her with hesitation and regret in his eyes.

She wondered what could possibly be so awful, then took a deep breath. "I'd still want to know. . . ."

WHAT ARE *LOVESWEPT* ROMANCES?

They are stories of true romance and touching emotion. We believe those two very important ingredients are constants in our highly sensual and very believable stories in the *LOVESWEPT* line. Our goal is to give you, the reader, stories of consistently high quality that may sometimes make you laugh, sometimes make you cry, but are always fresh and creative and contain many delightful surprises within their pages.

Most romance fans read an enormous number of books. Those they truly love, they keep. Others may be traded with friends and soon forgotten. We hope that each *LOVESWEPT* romance will be a treasure—a "keeper." We will always try to publish

LOVE STORIES YOU'LL NEVER FORGET
BY AUTHORS YOU'LL ALWAYS REMEMBER

The Editors

LOVESWEPT® • 491

Mary Kay McComas

Asking for Trouble

BANTAM BOOKS
NEW YORK • TORONTO • LONDON • SYDNEY • AUCKLAND

ASKING FOR TROUBLE

A Bantam Book / August 1991

If you would be interested in receiving protective vinyl covers for your Loveswept books, please write to this address for information:

Loveswept
Bantam Books
P.O. Box 985
Hicksville, NY 11802

ISBN 0-553-44146-9

Published simultaneously in the United States and Canada

Bantam Books are published by Bantam Books, a division of Bantam Doubleday Dell Publishing Group, Inc. Its trademark, consisting of the words "Bantam Books" and the portrayal of a rooster, is Registered in U.S. Patent and Trademark Office and in other countries. Marca Registrada. Bantam Books, 666 Fifth Avenue, New York, New York 10103.

PRINTED IN THE UNITED STATES OF AMERICA

OPM 0 9 8 7 6 5 4 3 2 1

For my aunts:
Betty Godbey, who plucked me out of the Perry horde and made me feel like someone special.
And Jean Rhines, who was there when I needed her the most and when my mother couldn't be.
Thank you both.

My love to Pa Kettle and my favorite Mason as well. . . .

One

"Wasn't living it bad enough? Why do I have to talk about it?" Sydney Wiesman asked her best friend, Judy.

"Because you've got to. It's part of the deal."

"I'll give back the money."

"You signed a contract," Judy said. In a low, reassuring whisper, she added, "Besides, this is your chance to find out how he really feels. Maybe he doesn't hate you."

"Maybe he does. Maybe he'll tell the whole world how much he hates me." Sydney moaned, wishing she'd never been born.

"You ready, Ms. Wiesman?" a young man wearing a large set of headphones asked, looking not at Sydney but at the clipboard in his hands.

"This is it, kiddo," Judy tittered in her ear, as she gave Sydney an enthusiastic hug. "Smile. It'll be fun. Really. And if he does get nasty, don't sit there like a ninny and cry. Fight back. There were two of you on that date, you know."

"You think he will? Get nasty?" Sydney asked,

suppressing the wail in her throat as she watched her friend scurry away.

Judy turned, backing her way along the long corridor. "No. I don't think he will. Stop worrying." She opened a door about halfway down the hall and disappeared inside.

"Do I really have to go through with this?" she asked the young man with a beseeching voice. "Isn't there some way to get out of it?"

He looked at her and grinned. "Come on, Ms. Wiesman, relax. Seven minutes, eight tops. You can do it. Don't worry."

Stop worrying? Don't worry? That was like telling Sydney not to breathe. Some people skied. Some people took up jogging. Her sport was worrying. She was an Olympic worrier. She could have had a career as a professional worrier. And at the moment, she was very, very nervous and very, very worried.

Sydney sighed, hard. Then she sighed again. Her stomach was so tight, she could play a drum solo on it.

"Okay, Ms. Wiesman. Just stand there and smile into the camera. Just the way we rehearsed it," the young man was saying before she realized that he had propped her up in front of a pale pink backdrop, that her segment of the program was about to begin, and that it was too late to back out.

"Oh, dear Lord," she prayed in despair, her hand on her stomach as it threatened to bring back up everything she'd eaten in the past year.

"Relax," he said again, "Rex'll take care of everything. He's done this hundreds of times, and he's a nice guy. He won't let anything awful happen to you. Now, after he introduces you, you turn and walk . . ."

Sydney listened to him review the stage directions for her, but only halfheartedly. She couldn't help but wonder if Tom Ghorman was as nervous as she was. The man had plagued her thoughts during the two weeks since their date. The worst of it was, she was more than a little disappointed their date hadn't worked out. She'd liked Tom instantly. She'd actually felt herself falling in love with him a little. And then the world had simply come apart at the seams and destroyed any possibility for a relationship.

"Welcome to *Electra-Love* . . . ," she heard the recorded announcement begin.

"Oh, dear Lord," she began to pray again—for an earthquake this time.

". . . The game show where the whimsies of love meet the logic of technology, and where all the personal details of a first date are aired on nationwide television. Now, here's your host, Rex Swann!"

Sydney watched Rex Swann descending the steps at the back of the set. This was his third entrance for the day. With a change of clothes and a touch-up to his makeup, he was as fresh and energetic looking as he had been the first time.

The audience clapped and cheered on cue, and Rex greeted them with words she was too tense to comprehend. She looked back at the camera in time to see the red light go on. Again she sent a prayer heavenward. *Please let the tightness around my mouth be a smile, not a grimace.*

"Let's welcome our first guest," she heard Rex say. "She's a CPA who enjoys sailing and long walks on the beach. She loves to dance and she's willing to try anything once. She's looking for a man with something to say, and her name is Sydney Wiesman. Come on over here, Sydney," Rex said, holding out a calm, stable hand to Sydney.

Like a well-programmed robot, she turned away from the camera and automatically began to walk toward Rex Swann. He was a handsome, affable-looking man with a good-natured twinkle in his eyes. The sort of man one felt compelled to trust. He took Sydney's hand.

"How are you doing, Sydney?" he asked in a low, confidential voice.

"I think I'm going to throw up," she whispered.

"You what?"

"I'm very nervous."

"No. No. Don't throw up," he said in a voice that was only slightly louder, but which most certainly could be picked up by the sound boom overhead. "There's nothing to be nervous about. Take a seat."

He pulled her over to center stage, to the rose-colored chair and loveseat where she would have to retell her nightmare. He patted her hand and smiled charmingly, sincerely concerned with her discomfort.

"Now, Sydney. You said you wanted a man who had something to say. What did you mean by that?" he asked, his smile encouraging.

"Well, Rex—" she had to stop and clear her tight, squeaky voice. "I'd like to talk about topics other than my work or his work. I'd like to meet someone I could talk to about a lot of different things, on a lot of different levels."

"Well, sure," he agreed. "We all know what it's like to be out after dark with the brain-dead." The audience laughed, and he gave them a wry smile. "You like to sail, take long walks on the beach, and dance. Would you say that you're a little bit of a romantic?"

"A little bit, sure."

"So, you're looking for a romantic man with a brain. What about a sense of humor, Sydney?"

"That'd be nice too, Rex," she said, wondering how Tom Ghorman's sense of humor had held up over the past couple of weeks. It was one of the things she had especially liked about him.

"Okay. Well, let's take a look at the men Sydney had to choose from, and then we'll find out who she chose and what happened on their date."

Everyone's attention turned to the large television screen located stage right, behind Rex.

"First there was Broylin, a motorcycle enthusiast, who says he prefers women with thick thighs and a lot of money," Rex read from the cue card, chuckling gleefully. A video of the monosyllabic Broylin saying basically the same thing played on the big screen.

"Then there's Humphrey. He's an avid bird-watcher and performs magic tricks as a clown for children's parties in his spare time. He wants a woman who can sit quietly for long periods of time without having to go to the bathroom, and here's why . . ."

Humphrey explained in a whiny voice how his dream woman was someone who could share his interest in bird-watching. His description of her would have better fit a rock.

"And then Tom, who says he'd like to start a family, if he could find the right woman to start it with," Rex reported. "This is what Tom's looking for . . ."

Sydney held her breath when she saw Tom's face on the video screen. She was reminded of why she'd picked him. Compared with the others, he was like a diamond to two pieces of coal. Compared with the rest of the male population in Sydney's acquaintance, he was still like a diamond, to hundreds of pieces of coal. He truly was a handsome man.

"I'd like to meet a warm, gentle woman who likes kids and who wants to share a life with someone like me," he said openly and honestly. "She could either pursue her career or stay home and raise the children, whichever made her happiest. But I think she'd have to be a very understanding person, because my profession can sometimes be a little stressful, and, well, she'd have to try to understand it."

The data on his videotape read: Tom Ghorman. Thirty-six. Human Services. Divorced.

That was all she'd known about him when she'd picked him. She knew more about him now. Understanding was indeed something he'd needed—and she had failed him miserably.

"Those are the three men Sydney had to choose from," Rex said. "And now it's time for the audience to vote on which of the three they'd pick for her."

The audience laughed, called out their preferred numbers, and voted. The bright stage lights and Sydney's nerves sent beads of perspiration trickling down her back and between her breasts.

"Now, Sydney, tell the audience and the folks at home who you picked for your date," Rex instructed her.

"I picked Tom."

On the screen behind Rex, Tom's face appeared again, just as she'd known it would. But this time he was backstage—not two hundred feet away. Worse yet, he could see her too, on the monitor in front of him.

"Hi, Tom. Nice to meet you. Are you comfortable back there?"

"Yes, very. Nice to meet you, Rex." He hesitated and then he added, "Hi, Sydney."

"Hi, Tom," she muttered, her heart pounding in

her throat, tears seeping into the corners of her eyes. She felt a sudden sense of . . . what? Relief? Well-being? And just as suddenly she knew that she'd missed him in the time they'd spent apart. She was profoundly glad to see him.

She welcomed the strange, airy sensation she got when she looked at him and the familiar fluttering of her heart when he smiled. She'd liked those feelings. She'd felt empty without them.

"Okay, Sydney. We'll let you start," Rex said, squirming with anticipation. "Did you call Tom?"

"Yes, Rex. I did call Tom," she said, her words stilted from anxiety.

"Well? What'd you think of him when you talked to him?"

Sydney almost laughed. She imagined that Rex would have liked to use a cattle prod on contestants like her, even though he didn't give any evidence of it. She looked up at Tom and took a deep breath to calm herself. She had faith in Tom. He was a nice man, a good man. He hadn't failed her; she had failed him. But she wouldn't fail him again by making them look like a couple of idiots on television, she decided.

"I thought he was funny," she said, smiling up at Tom.

"Funny strange, or funny ha-ha?" Rex asked.

"Ha-ha. Tom has a wonderful sense of humor," she said, as the muscles in her neck and back began to relax.

"Well, good. Then what happened? You got together."

Sydney laughed aloud this time. "Actually, Tom was twenty-four hours late for our date."

"No! Tom, how did that happen?" Rex made a horrendous face at the audience, they laughed, and then he turned in his seat to look up at Tom. "Twenty-four hours?"

Tom was grinning good-naturedly. The incident had happened early in their relationship. It was the first mishap, a simple misunderstanding that had been awkward, but not fatal. It was something they could both laugh about in retrospect.

"It's true, Rex," Tom said. At the sound of his deep, warm voice little chills ran up and down Sydney's back until she was forced to press it against the padding behind her. "Sydney made all the arrangements. We'd planned to meet at a restaurant, and I'd told Sydney that the twenty-third would be fine, thinking that the twenty-third was a Friday, a weekend night. Well," he continued, "the twenty-third was a Thursday. I'd even ordered flowers to be delivered to the restaurant on Friday."

Rex glanced at Sydney with a curious, sympathetic look on his face. "What did you do, Sydney? What did you think when Tom didn't show up?"

"I'd gone to the restaurant Thursday night, Rex. I waited for Tom to show up. Then I finally went home and called him to find out what had happened. I thought he'd gotten cold feet and decided not to go through with it, and I wasn't sure what to do. He felt really terrible," she said, laughing as she remembered his profuse apologies.

"So you ironed everything out and made other arrangements?"

"For the next night, yes."

"I picked Sydney up at her office," Tom said from the screen behind Rex. "Sydney's car was in the shop, which was one of the reasons why she'd wanted to meet on Thursday—so she'd have a getaway car if the date was horrible. The other reason was that she'd known she was going to have to work late that Friday night."

"Okay, so you got there. What happened after that?"

Tom looked down at the monitor and Sydney looked up at the screen behind Rex Swann. Through a maze and tangle of electrical wires and circuits, they shared one last moment of private, intimate exchange. Regret and sorrow passed between them, and so did resignation with the cosmic forces that had a tendency to clash and riot when the two of them were together.

The confusion with the day of the date had been a warning from the gods that Tom and Sydney were incompatible. Together they were the matter-antimatter paradox Scotty was always complaining about on *Star Trek*. They were the Bermuda Triangle, the black hole in the universe, and all the other catastrophic mysteries of life. Separately they functioned just fine, or so it had seemed.

Of course, neither one of them had suspected the forces their coming together would unleash. As a matter of fact, in the beginning, the forces they generated were pretty wonderful. . . .

Two

"Sydney?"

"Tom?" Sydney bounced out of her chair at the sound of his voice in the next room. She fluffed up her short brown curls with her fingers, moistened her lips with the tip of her tongue, and smoothed down the clean, simple lines of the pink linen suit she'd changed into earlier. She was halfway to the door before she missed her shoes and dashed back to her desk. Seconds later, with a welcoming smile on her face, she swung wide the partially opened door to her office.

The smile froze on her lips. Excitement stuck in her throat. The videotape had shown a washed-out imitation of the real Tom Ghorman. In person, he was much more . . . vivid, more lifelike and vital. Virile described the man in the videotape. There were no words to describe the sexy, raw maleness of the real Tom Ghorman; none to explain the elated, edgy, almost primal feeling he stirred in her.

Tom returned her smile. He was relieved to be in

the right place at the right time at last and more than relieved by what he saw.

Tom was a hunch man. He'd talked to her twice over the phone and had been willing to bet his last dollar that the woman on the other end of the line looked as alluring and seductive as her low, throaty voice. And she did.

The excruciating moment when two strangers meet and covertly—or not so covertly—inspect, study, and judge the other dragged on.

Sydney's gaze darted across Tom's broad shoulders and chest, took note of his lack of a beer belly, his slim hips, and the length and strength of his legs. She was pleased to see that he'd worn socks and dress shoes with his gray slacks and navy sport jacket, instead of slipping his bare feet into dockers for the sake of chic.

Tom, on the other hand, let loose a long, low whistle and grinned at her the way a wolf would a lamb. Sydney was a long-stemmed all-American beauty. Her hair fairly bounced with good health, her green, almond-shaped eyes shimmered with excitement and enthusiasm. And her skin . . . her skin looked petal soft with a fine rosy hue that came naturally from within.

"I sure hope you're Sydney Wiesman," he said. "I'm going to be real disappointed if you're not."

Sydney giggled, and then she wanted to kick herself. She'd planned to act sophisticated and cultured. She'd wanted to give him the impression that dating handsome men was a routine part of her life. She'd wanted to appear relaxed and confident, but the truth was, she was nervous as hell.

"I'm Tom Ghorman," he said. He took several steps forward and held out a friendly hand. The urge to touch her was so sharp, he could taste it, and he knew right away that a handshake wasn't going to cut it, but his options were restricted to the socially acceptable at the moment.

"I know," she said, forcing herself to take his hand. "I recognized you . . . and . . . and your voice." It had a tendency to send tickling shivers up her spine and make goose bumps on her arms.

His touch all but buckled her knees. She tolerated it for what she hoped was an appropriate amount of time, and then commanded her fingers—several times—to release his hand.

"That's right. I keep forgetting that you have a slight advantage," he said.

"I do?" Lord, she was glad to hear the news, but at a loss as to what the advantage was.

"You watched my tape and knew what I looked like."

"Well, yes, but . . ." She bit down sharply on the words "it didn't do you justice," and quickly substituted, ". . . but I couldn't see how tall you were."

"Or if I had a hunchback or a pot belly?" He smiled as he once again took slow inventory of all her best body parts. "I was afraid you'd have a wart on the end of your nose. But I hadn't exactly planned on your being beautiful either."

Sydney laughed breathlessly. Inside, she felt as if she were running the final distance in a marathon. Racing, racing, racing.

"Thank you," she murmured. She hoped she wasn't babbling. She closed her eyes tightly against the possibility as she turned and walked to her desk.

There had to be some means of dealing with the way the man looked, and with the way he looked at her. She would have sworn his eyes were green on the video, but they were blue, as clear and deep and bright as a summer sky. Wherever his gaze touched her, she felt bathed in a heat that would normally require a sunscreen. And, alas, she had none. She was vulnerable and unprotected.

"We planned this really well," she said, making a poor effort at sounding detached. "I was just finishing up when I heard you."

"This is the big corporation you were telling me about? The one you're going to audit on Monday?" he asked as he followed her into the room, enjoying the subtle sway of her hips.

"Well, they're not all that big, just complicated. A mortuary chain with a list of charitable contributions longer than my arm, to a company-controlled trust fund. Automatically, the IRS gets suspicious." She chuckled at her thoughts and spoke them out loud. "Actually, I have to admit it does look a little suspicious. It looks as if they're either laundering money or burying people for free."

"And who ever heard of that, huh?" he asked, humor in his voice. "Dying's expensive."

"It is," she said in all seriousness, acutely uncomfortable with the subject. "And I could see one or two freebies a year for tax write-offs, but they do so many that if the rest of the enterprise wasn't doing well, they'd go out of business." In a whisper she added, "Which is why I think they're laundering money."

"And why they're going to get stiffed by the IRS?" he added in the same tone of voice, with a twinkle in his eyes.

Sydney groaned at his pun, but liked his quick, sharp humor. She gathered up her purse and was about to turn off the lamp at her desk when she heard him ask, "Do you like puns? I saw this great sign at a tire store on the way over here."

"What'd it say?" she asked, glad to have something other than tax codes to talk about.

"Underneath their low, low prices it said, We Skid You Not." He waved her through the door in front of him.

She chuckled and smiled. "I have a terrible time remembering punch lines. Do you like knock-knock jokes?" she asked, knowing that humor was a great way to break the ice with strangers, but wishing she had a more cultured selection of witticisms to choose from.

"Do frogs have tongues?" he answered. He was itching for a good excuse to touch her again. Indulgently, he placed a gentle guiding hand to the small of her back, deciding that the limits of acceptable social behavior were too narrow and a royal pain in the rear.

She was trying to remember if frogs did have tongues.

"I love knock-knock jokes," he said helpfully, fascinated by the rapid changes in her expression, eager to know the cause and meaning of her every move.

"Okay. Knock-knock."

"Who's there?"

"Crunch."

"Crunch who."

"God bless you."

The last three words hung in the air like a rain cloud about to burst. She looked at Tom, who was already staring down his nose at her. She shrugged, wishing she could hide under the wall-to-wall carpeting. "It was the only one I could remember. My nephew told it to me."

"Knock-knock," he said, his gaze wandering over her face.

"Who's there?" The question was real. She wanted to know who the man beside her was, with eyes so keen and clear they seemed to look straight into the heart of her.

"Mrs. Highwater."

"Mrs. Highwater who?"

"Mrs. Helen Highwater," he said, and then he grinned. "I have a nephew too."

"How old?" she asked, relaxing a little. Tom Ghorman was a nice man, she decided instantly. He'd had the chance to make her feel like a jerk and had let it slip by.

"Seven. He takes any chance he gets to use a forbidden word or say something dirty. The grosser the better."

"Like the book titles?" These were her nephew's favorites.

"Like *Under the Bandstands* by Seymour Butts?"

She groaned as the elevator doors opened. Sydney greeted a maintenance man by his first name as she stepped in beside Tom and pushed the button for the main floor. "What about Mister Completely?" Tom said. "He wrote—"

He stopped short when a loud squeaking noise came from above the elevator, and looked up at the lights over the door.

"Uh-oh," he said, struggling to appear calmer than he felt as he started pushing all the buttons on the selection panel one at a time.

"It's stuck." It was only a seven-story building, but Sydney had visions of them plummeting for miles to a horrible and gruesome death at the bottom of the elevator shaft. Panic rose up within her like a monster from a slimy green lagoon. "It's stuck. We can't get out. There's been another earthquake. The power's failed. We'll die in here before anyone finds us," she said all in one breath, as she reached over and hit the red alarm by reflex.

Tom took her by the shoulders and turned her toward him. He recognized the trapped and helpless fear in her, but knew better than to give it any latitude.

"Hear that," he yelled at her over the alarm. "It wouldn't work if there'd been a power failure. No earthquake either, or we'd have felt it before the elevator stopped. And we're not going to die in here, because somebody's bound to hear that noise."

"Right." She flashed him a smile for his brilliant logic and opened the little metal door on the panel that concealed the emergency telephone. She pulled the red knob to a stop position and into the silence spoke as if she hadn't been a raving lunatic moments before. "I'll just call maintenance and have someone come up and get us out."

"No need to do that," came a voice from the back of the elevator.

Both Tom and Sydney turned to look. The maintenance man stood with his hands on his belt full of tools, bouncing back and forth on the balls of his feet.

"Can't answer the phone right now. Things are a little up in the air," he said, and then he guffawed at his own humor.

"Can you fix the elevator?" Sydney asked, deceptively unruffled.

"Not from in here, Ms. Wiesman. Got to get to the circuit box, check the cables, stuff like that. Want a drink?" He pulled a shiny metal flask from his rear pocket and offered it to her.

"Ah . . . no, thank you. You're . . . um . . . ," she was afraid to say the words. "You're not the only maintenance man on duty tonight, are you?"

He offered the flask to Tom as he shook his head in dismay. "Weekends and nights, there's only one of us. Well, one of us and the girls who clean up."

"Can they do any anything to help us?"

"They could dust and vacuum in here, I guess," he said, dragging his index finger across the elevator wall before he took a swig from his flask, his eyes sparkling with good spirit.

Sydney took a menacing step toward him, fully prepared to do serious damage to the man's head and neck, when Tom caught her by the arm. Again he took note of the anger and desperation in her eyes, but he didn't address them. Instead, he looked back at the maintenance man and asked, "When's your shift over?"

"Midnight, but . . ."

"Midnight? But that's four hours from now. We'll suffocate," Sydney said, fear creeping into her voice again. Small spaces never bothered her. It was the locked-in part that was undermining her sanity. Being unable to get out of any space, large or small, played games with her mind and encouraged her hysteria.

"Nah. There's plenty of air in here," the man said.

"Can you call outside the building on this phone?" Tom asked, still holding on to Sydney's arm. "Or could we call one of the cleaning ladies and have her call out for help?"

"Nope. It's a direct line to our office in the basement, and they don't clean down there."

"What would happen if we left the alarm on?"

"We'd probably go deaf," the man said, as he lowered himself to the floor. "But it wouldn't get us outta here any quicker."

Sydney watched as he again removed the flask from his back pocket and began to loosen the top. Then she turned to look at Tom, who, to her complete exasperation, was loosening his tie and removing his jacket. He folded it neatly over the handrail on the wall and then joined the maintenance man on the floor.

"Do you know any good, fairly clean jokes?" Tom asked the man.

"This is insane!" she shouted, hands on her hips, her mind replaying the plummeting pictures. Didn't they know that there was no way out? How could they act so calm? Didn't they know the danger they were in? Hadn't they ever seen movies where the heroine hung by a single thread of wire for an indeterminate amount of time before she . . . plummeted. Addressing them both, she asked, "Aren't you going to *do* something?"

Tom looked up at her and smiled. "The elevator's stuck. What would you like us to do?"

"Get us out of here." The elevator seemed suddenly smaller than it had been when she'd first walked into it.

"Sydney," Tom said as if talking to a fearful child. "Are you all right? You look a little pale."

"Pale? Me? I can't get out of here. I'm going to be plummeting to my death any second now, with a maintenance man and a date from a television game show, who don't seem to realize the danger we're in. And I'm pale? Why should I be pale?" She turned back to the telephone and dialed 911 with a prayer on her lips.

"Sydney?" Tom's voice was as quiet and composed as an undertaker's. His arm circled her waist. His other hand covered hers over the receiver of the phone and helped her to replace it on the wall. "No one is going to answer the phone, but you don't need to worry. We're perfectly safe here. This man says . . ."

"Jerry," she said, her voice sounding dull in her ears. "His name is Jerry."

"Jerry says it's an electrical problem. He says this thing was inspected three weeks ago, and it's as strong and safe as it was the day they installed it. Isn't that right, Jerry?"

"Hell if I know. I wasn't here when they installed—"

"Isn't that right, Jerry?" Tom said, sending a quelling expression over his shoulder.

"Sure. You bet."

She trembled in his arms, which under any other circumstances would have pleased him. As it was, it stimulated his concern for her.

"See, Sydney? Now why don't you sit down here beside me and we'll talk and get to know each other better." He chuckled. "Actually, I was hoping we could be alone for a while tonight. Restaurants are always so crowded, and you have to be careful not to talk with your mouth full of food." With his hands on her elbows, he picked her up and turned her around as if she were a mannequin. "This'll be great. We can talk and have an extremely late dinner when . . . when we're finished," he said, choosing his words carefully.

"Want that drink now?" Jerry asked, extending the flask out to her.

Sydney managed to hold up a hand in refusal as she concentrated on lowering herself to the floor. Alcohol was the last thing she needed. She didn't handle it well, and she had her hands full already trying not to lose her mind.

Something in her realized that Tom was right, that there wasn't anything to do but wait. But the greater part of her was so filled with fear, she could hardly breathe.

"Maybe just a tiny sip?" she heard Tom saying in a soothing voice. He was seated next to her with one arm holding her close. He held Jerry's flask to her lips.

"Makes me silly," she said, shaking her head.

"That's okay. You could use a little silly right now," he said, as hot liquid scorched the back of her throat and burned its way to her abdomen. "You're so tense, I'm afraid you'll snap in two."

Coughing and sputtering, she placed her hands over his and pulled the flask away from her face. After the initial shock of the liquor, she simply sat there for several long minutes trying to gather her thoughts and some of her dignity.

How on earth did I get into this mess? she asked herself, trying hard to remember the exact reason why she'd done such an uncharacteristic thing as agreeing to be a game show contestant.

Six weeks earlier, Sydney had come home from a date drained and listless. Her roommate had glanced up from the late night game show she was watching on television and had commented frankly, "You look like hell."

"I feel like hell," Sydney had said, flopping down on the couch beside her. "There ought to be a law against CPAs dating each other. It breeds monotony and contempt, and it's mentally and spiritually retarding. It ought to be right up there with incest and . . . and . . . is marrying your first cousin the same as incest?"

"Yeah. I think so," Judy said, amazing Sydney with her ability to follow two conversations at once. She'd never looked away from the program. "This is what you should do, pal." She motioned to the TV. "I haven't seen one contestant that was a CPA in all the times I've watched it."

Sydney sat up and took interest.

"Great," she said after several minutes of watching the show, chewing on popcorn taken from Judy's bowl. "He's a musician and she's a mud wrestler. Who would they set me up with? A bull breeder?"

"They have yuppie types too. Architects, bank executives, lawyers. And where is it written that a bull breeder can't be a great date? It's not what they do that counts, you know, it's who they are. Accountants are born dull and sort of . . . linear. That's why they're good at what they do."

"Thank you so much," Sydney muttered, never having considered herself dull or linear. She reached for more popcorn.

"Well, what could it hurt? To go on this program, I mean." Judy took a fistful of popcorn and dropped it into her mouth a piece at a time. "You work late hours. On the rare occasions you do go out, you go to IRS seminars. The only men you ever meet are CPAs. You need some variety in your life."

This was no great revelation to Sydney. She knew she needed variety. But who had time for variety? And if one had the time, who felt like hanging out in singles bars and nightclubs filtering through the assortment to find just one man who was tolerable?

After a few days of deep deliberation Sydney had decided to try it. She'd called the studio, gone in for the interview, filled out the questionnaire, and within two weeks she'd gone to watch three computer-selected videotapes of men she could choose from before the taping of the game show.

Sydney had found the choice to be quite easy, actually, and only briefly wondered if it had been set up that way by the people at the studio. She'd picked the most handsome man of the three and the only one who had used complete sentences when he'd spoken. Tom Ghorman.

Sitting beside him—so near calamity—she refused to regret her actions. The game show was perhaps the greatest risk she'd ever taken in her life, and Tom Ghorman excited her more than any man she'd ever met. If she were about to die, it was good to know that in her brief existence she had taken at least one risk and that she was capable of feeling great excitement and arousal. She was thankful for that.

"I'm really sorry," she said at last, feeling weak all over. "I'm not claustrophobic. I just . . ."

"Hey. Don't worry about it," Tom said, smiling as she looked at him. "It's over. And if I didn't have you to impress with my male bravado, I'd be screaming and beating on ol' Jerry here. So, you see, we're helping each other."

Her tiny smile of gratitude seemed stingy in contrast to all he'd done for her. He was being very kind and extremely understanding. What must he think of her? Sydney wondered as she raised his hand and the flask to her lips once more.

"So, you two don't even know each other, huh?" Jerry commented as if it had finally sunk into his head. "Kind of a weird way to spend a first date."

Tom assisted Sydney with another sip from the flask as he answered, "Oh, I don't know. I'll bet if you gave ten men the choice of getting stuck in an elevator with a beautiful woman or going to the movies or a restaurant with her on a first date, nine of them would choose the elevator and the other one would be gay. I couldn't have planned this any better."

"You got a point there," Jerry agreed, watching his flask with a possessive eye. "Did I hear that you met on TV?"

While Tom explained the circumstances of their date, Sydney was busy taking note of her present situation. For instance, she decided the floor of the elevator was very comfortable. She especially liked leaning against Tom's broad chest and the way his hand brushed up and down her arm in a soothing, reassuring manner. He smelled good too.

When she kicked her shoes off and pulled her legs up under her, she found that if she scooted up just a bit, she could lay her head on his shoulder and watch his thick dark hair move against the collar of his shirt as he talked to Jerry. She wondered what it felt like, and what shampoo he used.

She started to wonder a lot about him, actually. He was in human services, according to his videotape. Did he control crazy women in defective elevators for a living? He looked good in blue too. Was it his favorite color? Should she have worn her blue satin dress instead of the pink linen? She'd asked her cat the night before, and after some hemming and hawing they'd finally decided on the pink, but what if he hated cats and would have preferred her in blue? He had nice hands, she noted, her mind shifting quickly, her attention span atypically short. Had he gone to college? Did he play a sport? He has such nice teeth, she thought, just before she speculated as to whether or not he'd worn braces. He was kind of funny too. . . .

"What *did* Mister Completely write?" she asked, coming suddenly to the party, her voice a little louder than usual though she was feeling amazingly relaxed and jolly.

Jerry and Tom looked at her as if she'd just returned after a long absence. Tom glanced at the flask still clutched in their hands and then back at Sydney, assessing her carefully.

"The joke, remember? When we first got on the

elevator? What book did Mister Completely write?"

"*Hole in the Mattress.*"

She snorted a giggle through her nose and then laughed aloud as Jerry and Tom exchanged knowing glances and began to laugh too.

"Maybe we can give this back to Jerry now," Tom said, slipping the flask from her fingers. "You seem to be feeling better."

"I do," she said, more proud than amazed. "Let's tell more jokes."

Tom's chuckle made his chest vibrate, and when he gave her shoulders an affectionate squeeze, she sighed and felt warm and happy all over.

She liked Tom Ghorman. He wasn't stuffy and number oriented like most of her dates. He laughed as easily as he breathed, and nothing, including the fact that she might be a little tipsy, seemed to bother him. He didn't even know that she was a senior manager with the firm, and he liked her anyway, accepted her for who she was. She really did like Tom Ghorman.

"You're okay for a girl, Sydney Wiesman," he said in a low voice, much the way his nephew might, but with a certain admiration in his eyes that only an adult male could bestow.

She wanted Tom Ghorman to like her too. Not enough to pretend to be someone she wasn't, but absolutely enough to be flattered by his praise.

She enjoyed the way his gaze lingered on her legs, or drifted down to her mouth, or further down across the curves of her breasts and hips when he thought she wasn't looking. It made her feel pretty and feminine. Oh, she knew sexual attraction wasn't the most important aspect of a relationship, but she was undeniably human and ingrained with the notion that a little healthy sex appeal never hurt anyone.

She took a deep breath, filling her senses with Tom's scent. There was no thick, cloying aroma, no perfume that was sweet enough or strong enough to gag a horse. It was simply a light, mysterious musky smell that fascinated her.

Three

The three of them sat on the floor of the elevator regaling one another with their repertoire of jokes, and she soon discovered that what she liked best about Tom was his laugh. She went out of her way to hear it over and over again.

"So the new hillbilly dogcatcher stepped forward and said, 'The reason I ain't caught no dogs yet, is cuz I don't know what I'm 'posed to catch 'em at.'" Sydney articulated in her best hillbilly dialect.

Tom's laugh, low and rumbling, filled the elevator with cozy good cheer and did queer things to Sydney's pulse. She got the distinct feeling that he was laughing more at the way she told the joke than the joke itself, but it didn't really matter.

Jerry's prediction that there would be plenty of air to breathe in the elevator seemed to be true. Actually, it had been some time since she'd given it any thought. And if she pretended very hard that she could open the doors anytime she wished, she found the sight of their firmly closed surface almost tolerable.

But between the hot air they were blowing at one

another and the fact that the air-conditioning was somehow involved with the elevator malfunction, the small enclosed box had become an oven. She had long since removed her jacket and released the tail of her camisole-style top from the waistband of her skirt.

When she'd finished with her series of hillbilly jokes and passed the limelight on to Jerry, she leaned back against the wall again and was gratified to feel Tom's arm still behind her. The warmth of his skin beneath his shirtsleeve and the tight power of his arm against her bare back were like candy—sweet, forbidden, and too tempting to resist. In no distress at the moment, however, she felt obliged to sit forward to release him, but his hand curled around her upper arm and held her steady.

He acted as if sitting with his arm around a near total stranger, his hand brushing lightly over her skin and driving her nuts with tiny tingles, were the most natural thing in the world. But it didn't feel natural to Sydney. It was something new and enlivening, something she wanted to investigate further.

Every time she moved beside him, every time he felt her take a deep breath and sigh, it was an erotic torment. He wanted to touch her. He longed to feel the texture and warmth of her skin with the tips of his fingers, against his naked body and in his mind. He had a yen to lower her gently onto her back and make love to her slowly, thoroughly, until she screamed in ecstasy.

She looked at him, but he pretended to be listening to Jerry. Countless times he'd caught himself staring at her. She was going to start thinking he was perverted if he wasn't more careful, he thought. But he couldn't get over the feeling that he'd seen her before somewhere. Not really *seen* her, on the street or in the newspaper or at a party. But seen in a visualized sense, like in a dream or a fantasy. Yep. The more he labored over it, the more certain he became that he had known her before, that she'd stepped out of his fondest dream.

Jerry, due either to his limited supply of clean jokes or his seemingly limitless supply of liquid spirits, introduced several ribald stories before Tom switched the evening's entertainment to humorous personal anecdotes.

She wasn't sure if his story about a championship football game in high school was meant to be extremely long and tedious, but there was a smile on his lips when Jerry fell asleep, lolling to one side for several minutes before he finally toppled over onto the floor, snoring atrociously.

"Don't you just hate a third wheel?" he asked, turning his full attention to Sydney.

"I do," she said, smiling nervously over at the sleeping maintenance man. She felt like an astronaut during countdown, eager to see space and land on the moon, but aware of the dangers along the way. "Although you might still be trying to scrape me off the ceiling if it weren't for him and his handy little flask. I'm really sorry about that."

"Don't be. Are you feeling better?" He was sure she couldn't look any better.

"Yes. Hungry is all."

"Mm. Me too." He tilted his head back against the wall and closed his eyes, pulling Sydney a tad closer. "Where will we go when we get out of here, and what will we eat?"

"At midnight? Oh! I know," she said with a jolt of enthusiasm. "There's an all-night diner about three miles from here, off the boulevard. It has the greatest grease burgers I've ever eaten."

He opened his eyes and smiled at her. "Will you marry me?"

"What?"

"You have to be the last woman in California who isn't a health food freak, repulsed by the mere thought of a grease burger. We were made for each other."

She laughed. "Actually, I'm a recovering junk-food-aholic. I know it's bad for me, and I try to eat better food, but once in a while I go on these binges and . . . well, it's too embarrassing to talk about."

"No, no. Tell me more. What else am I going to like about you?"

"I don't know. I don't know you well enough to know what you like."

"I like beautiful women."

She could tell it was true by the way he was staring at her. Her cheeks burned, and she wanted to giggle like a schoolgirl. Instead she said, "Not me. I'm into good-looking men. Do you enjoy going to the beach?"

"I love the beach. I live close to the marina, *and*"—he wagged his brows up and down—"I own a schooner you might be interested in."

"I love to sail."

"I know. You told me the other night on the phone. I figured that if you didn't like me, I might be able to hold your interest if I bribed you with an afternoon of sailing."

"It would have worked," she said, smiling. But they both knew that it wouldn't be necessary. "This is very strange. What else do we have in common?"

The list seemed endless. Neither one was much

of a party person, though they both had friends they enjoyed spending time with. They enjoyed movies in movie theaters as opposed to videos, and they both liked to read—although she preferred biographies and he science fiction. They argued briefly over the death penalty and abortion laws before they agreed not to talk religion or politics until they knew each other better. Then their words grew serious.

"Do you eat crackers in bed?" he asked, straightening the thin spaghetti strap that had fallen off her shoulder, savoring—at last—the smooth, silky warmth of her skin.

Jerry let loose a grunting noise. They chuckled together, but she couldn't displace the knowledge that his fingers had moved on and were tracing the curves at the base of her neck.

"Crackers? Ah, if I'm sick and I'm eating soup too, I sometimes eat them in bed. But not on a routine basis, no. Do you?" They'd been asking these sorts of questions for some time, a get-to-know-you game with no rules and no holds barred.

"No. Do you . . . like hot or warm showers?" he asked, his finger traveling back down the line of the strap.

She swallowed hard and tried to remember—no easy task while little shivers raced up her neck and across her breasts.

"Ah, warm in the morning, hot to relax, and cool to cool off when it's hot," she said, wondering if she'd made sense. "What about you?"

"Hot."

His gaze met hers. Hot. Oh, yes. Sydney could see very well that the man liked *everything* hot. He was not a tepid man. He would have his food spicy, his women flushed and sultry, his passions fiery, and his sex torrid and frenzied.

Again a twinge of anxiety pulled at her. She'd prayed for someone more exciting than the quiet, sedate CPAs she'd been dating, but she wasn't sure if she was ready for a man like Tom Ghorman. He was looking at her as if he could eat her alive—no, he was looking at her as if he wanted to make her *feel* alive.

The message in his eyes made her heart pump so fast, there was no distinguishing one beat from the next. There was air locked deep in her lungs that she couldn't get out. She felt ready to explode.

"Do you sleep on your back or your stomach?" he asked, his voice hardly more than a whisper, his face extremely close to hers. A kiss. That's what he wanted now. Touching her was all he'd hoped it would be, a new high in tactile pleasure. But it wasn't enough. A kiss, now that would be something, he calculated.

"I . . . sleep on my side. My left side. And I hardly mess up the sheets. I don't think I move all night," she said, rushing once she got started. "Do you snore?"

"I've been accused of breathing loud, but not snoring."

"Where . . . how do you sleep? The position, I mean," she stammered, as he lowered his eyes to watch his finger skimming across the top of her blouse, grazing the soft fullness of her breasts.

"All over the bed. And I make a mess of the sheets." She should have known he'd say that, she thought. He probably put a lot of energy into everything he did. "I do miss sleeping with a woman, though."

"That's right," she said, grabbing at the information. "I'd forgotten that you're divorced. How long has it been?"

"Seven years."

She couldn't help it, she was astounded. "You haven't had sex in seven years?"

He laughed and shook his head once. "That's not what I said. There's a huge difference between sleeping with someone and having sex with them."

"Well, sure. When you're sleeping, you're sleeping. And when you're not . . . you're, ah, not."

He fingered the strap on her other shoulder, and while she turned to putty, he said, "When you sleep with someone you can roll over in the middle of the night and know you're not alone. When it's cold you can cuddle up to that person and sleep like a baby. You can wake her up and talk when you're worried or afraid. You can have sex with anyone, but you need someone special to sleep with."

"And your wife was someone special?"

"In the beginning. That's when I first made the distinction, I suppose. But by the time we'd been married eighteen months, we were sleeping in different beds . . . in different houses . . . with different people."

"She cheated on you?" Sydney found this hard to believe. How could any woman risk losing a man like Tom?

He looked surprised. "How do you know it was her? What makes you think it wasn't me?"

She shrugged. He didn't seem the type. He gave her the impression of being someone who was possessive, but also faithful once he'd made up his mind on a partner. But how could she explain an impression? "Because you enjoyed sleeping with her, I guess. Anyone that content in their marriage wouldn't have to cheat."

He smiled at her perceptiveness and toyed with the tiny silver loop in her earlobe. Sydney was someone special, someone he could sleep with, he knew instinctively. Of course, sex with her wouldn't be too shabby either, he decided with his second thought.

"Actually," he said, "we were separated before she started sleeping around, and I hadn't cared about what she was doing for months before that, so it didn't really matter."

"Not a very long marriage," she muttered, more to herself than to Tom. She was wondering what had happened for him to go from discovering the joys of sleeping with his wife to total disinterest in less than eighteen months.

"No, but it was long enough for me to realize that I liked being married and what kind of woman I'd need to make it last."

It was on the tip of her tongue to ask about this wonder woman he was looking for, but she held the words back. If anything was going to happen between them, she wanted it to happen honestly. If she knew what he thought a perfect woman was, it would be too easy to take on those qualities to please him. She wanted him to want Sydney.

"You're lucky," she said. "All I know is what I don't want."

"Which is?"

Her thoughts would sound mean and cruel if she voiced them, so she hesitated, looking for kinder words.

"It's hard to explain," she said, looking away. He fiddled with the short hairs along the nape of her neck, scrambling her thoughts, making speech almost impossible. "I don't know how . . . to explain it, except that my mother always says that when I meet the right man, I'll know it in my heart. And . . . and the men I've been dating have left my heart disappointed and bored and angry. Disappointed because they're not the man I'm looking for. Bored because I'm not interested in them.

Angry because they're not telling my heart what it wants to hear. And it's not their fault. They're nice men. They're just not *my* man. Does that make sense?"

As she looked at him his fingers closed around the back of her neck. He had a curious expression on his face—gentle, decisive, and passionate at once. He tipped his head and pressed his lips to hers.

Her heart caught in her throat while something else fluttered in her chest and her insides tied themselves in knots. He tasted her lips with the tip of his tongue, and she felt his hand slide around her waist to pull her closer. She surrendered to his mouth and tongue as he deepened the kiss.

A kiss? Is that what he'd been wanting from her all this time? A kiss? Touching his lips to Sydney's wasn't like any kissing he'd done before. It was . . . Lord, how to explain it? It was intimate. Something warm and private, a carnal secret, thorough and erotic beyond his wildest imaginings. Addictive. Consuming.

Her mind drifted in a land of clouds and castles. He drew the air from her lungs. Her breasts became engorged with desire. He crushed her against the thick, hard muscles of his chest, and she felt as if she'd been swept off the ground. Her heart soared. She knew the sun and the wind and the stars.

Tom had her face in his hands when he pulled away. She took in a tremulous breath and stared into skylike eyes that knew where she'd been, what she'd seen, and how she'd felt.

"Oh my," she muttered, moving away as she tried to catch her breath. She felt intensely exposed and out of her element. Tom let his hands slip into his lap and didn't try to keep her near.

She glanced at him and was relieved to see that he was watching her with a warmhearted smile.

"I can't believe how close I came to not going through with this," he said, as if awed by the wonders of the universe. If she was as shaken as he by the enormity of what they had discovered, he wanted to put her at ease. The last thing he wanted to do was scare her away. "It was a buddy's idea originally. He got hooked on the program and was telling me about it one night. We were laughing and making jokes. You know, describing the women we'd probably end up with." He chuckled in recollection. "Then out of the blue he said I should go down for an interview and get on the show. Now I'm going to have to apologize for laughing at him and calling him crazy."

She smiled at the familiarity of his story and asked, "What made you change your mind?"

"I don't know. Right up until that first afternoon when you called and introduced yourself, I was planning to back out."

"Why didn't you?"

"I liked your voice," he said, a strange light appearing in the depths of his eyes. It was more than her voice now. It was her face, the way her mind worked, the way she laughed. . . .

"I liked yours too." Their gazes met, and there was a brief tussle of wills, his beckoning and hers shying away, until she was forced to look elsewhere.

It was happening too fast. A champion worrier, she needed time to think and stew about the emotions he stirred in her. Were they simply physical? Were they supposed to come this quickly? Invade her so deeply? Could two people fall in love in an elevator in less than four hours? Was that her heart or her loneliness speaking to her?

She screamed and jumped when the elevator phone rang, but was quick to get on her feet and answer on the second ring.

"Hello?"

"Hello," came a man's voice. "Is this the elevator?"

"Yes. Is this the other maintenance man?"

"Charlie Levitz here. Who are you?"

"I'm Sydney Wiesman. I work on the seventh floor. I'm with Danbury Associates. Tom and Jerry and I have been stuck in this elevator since just after eight o'clock tonight. Can you get us out, please?"

"Who did you say was in there with you?" he asked.

"Tom and Jerry."

"The cat and the mouse?"

"What?"

"You know." He laughed. "The cat and the mouse. Tom and Jerry. Get it? It's a joke."

"What a comedian, Mr. Levitz." She shifted her weight from one foot to the other impatiently. "How long do you think it will take to get us out of here?"

With the man's solemn promise to have them out in less than thirty minutes, she hung up the phone feeling pensive and a little sad. What would happen now that she and Tom were about to be rescued? Would everything change? Would freedom dilute the strength of the emotions they'd felt in the confined space of the elevator? Worriers worried about such things, she knew.

She turned and gasped when she discovered that Tom had come up behind her, blocking her into the corner with his body.

"Let's call him back and tell him to forget about fixing the elevator," he said, probing her thoughts with his gaze, inviting her to spend more time alone with him. "I don't want this date to end yet."

"Oh, it can't end yet," she said on a bright note, her body humming with anticipation. "They gave me money to pay for it. We can't go home until we've spent it. It's one of the rules."

It wasn't exactly a written rule, but who'd want to have to give all the money back and admit on national television that the date never happened?

"Well, thank heaven for rules," he said, the desire in his eyes drugging her mind like a potent narcotic.

When he kissed her, her arms automatically wound themselves around his neck, and her body instinctively pressed close to his. Kissing him was natural. There was nothing to study or assemble. It didn't feel contrived. She simply submitted to her own will, and her emotions took over.

A horrendous snort and grunt from the drunken heap of pliers and wrenches on the floor was enough to distract the dead. To those very much among the living, but spellbound in a state of bliss, the noise was a minor disturbance.

Tom held her tight, reluctant to let the moment pass.

Sydney was glowing inside. She cleared her mind of all the *what ifs* that cluttered her life and wallowed in the new and marvelous sensations of what was.

"We should wake our friend up," Tom said, willfully setting her an arm's distance away. "I feel as if I owe him that much, just for going to sleep."

Twenty minutes later, the three of them were alert, tucked in, and standing in front of the door with jackets and tool belt in hand, waiting for the elevator to move. Sydney took deep breaths as a familiar panic churned in her abdomen. *The doors will open, the doors will open,* she told herself over and over.

There were several false starts as the cables clattered and squeaked overhead. The elevator bounced portentously before it finally made a slow descent to the first floor and released its prisoners.

"Well, it was nice to meet you, Tom," Jerry said, when they'd regrouped after long turns at the water fountain and mad dashes to the restrooms. He'd already thanked them both repeatedly for waking him up. "Maybe I'll see you again sometime."

"There's always that possibility," Tom replied, with a glance in Sydney's direction.

"What was it you said you did for a living?"

"Ah . . . I'm in human services," Tom said, faltering.

"What kind of human services?"

"Oh, you know, the usual kind," he said. He shrugged and made a vague gesture with his hand. This wasn't the right time to be talking about his job. He was fast falling in love with Sydney, but in truth he barely knew her. "Listening to problems, paperwork, that sort of thing . . . ," he said, leading Sydney toward the main door with a firm grip on her elbow.

"You work down at the welfare office?" Jerry called. "Because I'm down there once in a while with my sister when her car don't work and maybe we could—"

"No. Not in the welfare office." He pushed Sydney through the door and then turned back to the maintenance man. "Look, Jerry. The next time I see you, it'll be right here in this building. I plan to come here a lot."

Jerry grinned, waved, and ambled off with Charlie toward the stairwell.

"What sort of human services *do* you perform?" Sydney asked, waiting on the sidewalk for him to catch up with her.

"The kind nobody likes to do without," he said, sliding his arm around her waist and pulling her to him so he could give her a quick peck on the lips. "My car's over this way."

She let him steer her around down the block, still wondering what he did for a living.

"And what kind of human service is it that nobody likes to do without?"

He arched a brow and gave her a licentious stare. "You want a demonstration?"

Before she could answer, before she had time to even decide if she wanted a demonstration or not, he took her into his arms and gave her a kiss that was deep, sweet, and long.

"Gigolo?" she murmured against his lips at her first opportunity.

"For you, I'm free." He kissed her again.

Soon she didn't care what he did, as long as he saved enough time for kissing. Still . . . "Really. What do you do?" she asked as they walked hand in hand, hardly noticing the traffic on the busy boulevard.

"Don't you just hate talking about your job on a date?" he asked. "Let's save job talk for when we've run out of other things to talk about. How long do you think it'll take us?"

She hoped forever. Her prime complaint with her usual dates had been the lack of topics for discussion. She was sick of job talk and more than willing to comply with his suggestion.

"Forever, I hope."

"Dammit it to hell!"

"What?" she cried, startled by his sudden outburst. She watched in confusion and amazement as he paced the sidewalk and ran a hand through his hair in an agitated fashion.

"I don't believe it! This is the second time in a year this has happened to me!" he shouted to the world. "Why me? The insurance company isn't going to believe this. *I* don't believe this. What is it with those guys? Why don't they make it a once-in-a-lifetime experience for *everybody* instead of picking on me all the time? Dammit, this makes me so mad."

"What? Tom, what is it?" Sydney asked again, wondering if she'd dare touch him. She wanted to do something to help, but she wasn't sure what.

"My car. Do you see my car?" He motioned to the empty curb space. "I parked it here. Do you see it now?"

"Ah, no." He gave her a does-that-answer-your-question look and continued to pace. Thinking quickly, she said, "But that doesn't necessarily mean it's been stolen. Maybe it was towed. Maybe the police thought it was an abandoned car and had it towed away."

"Who the hell would abandon a forty-thousand-dollar car, Sydney?" he shouted at her.

Sydney marched twenty feet down the sidewalk to a signpost and then shouted right back. "The idiot who parked it in a two-hour zone and then got stuck in an elevator for four, is my best guess."

Either the tone of her voice or her remarkably sound logic made him stop pacing. She saw a new light of respect in his eyes, and she liked it.

"Is it really a two-hour zone?" he asked, sheepishly.

"Would I lie to you?"

"I don't know," he said, much to her surprise.

He had the nerve to walk over and look at the

sign himself. And then he grinned at her, teasing her with his eyes. So she hit him in the arm.

"Okay," he said, laughing. "There's a chance it was towed. We're still without wheels, and we're both starving."

They watched each other think for a few seconds and then Sydney offered her plan. "We'll call a taxi."

"Great idea. You got a phone in your purse?"

"No," she said very sweetly, grinning back at him. "But there's one in the lobby of my building, and if you go back and ring the service bell, Jerry or Charlie will let you in to use it."

"Brains *and* beauty." He sighed loudly. "Please say you'll marry me."

"Will you go? I'm so hungry, I could eat this sign."

He started to jog off, then stopped and turned around. "Come with me."

"Are you scared?"

"Yes. I don't want you wandering off while I'm gone." He looked at the traffic passing by and the darkened buildings surrounding them. "This isn't the best place in the world for a beautiful woman with brains to be alone, either."

"Well, thank you, but I'll be fine. I work late all the time. This street isn't new to me."

"Sure?"

"Go."

Four

Sydney watched Tom until he turned toward the building and disappeared behind the ornamental shrubbery near the entrance. She enjoyed every second of it.

The man had a wonderful body—tall, lean, muscular. She sighed and swung around the signpost by one hand. If she was falling in love, she hoped she'd never hit bottom. He was more than she'd ever dreamed her someone would be. Handsome, intelligent, witty, charming . . .

"Hey, mama! What you doin' out here alone by yourself?"

Sydney groaned and glanced over at a beat-up car full of teenagers, then immediately wished she hadn't. One of them was hanging by his armpits through the open window, ogling her, while his three or four companions encouraged him.

Slowly, calmly, she turned and began walking back to her office building. Tom had surely had enough time to summon Jerry and/or Charlie to the lobby. A group of boys wouldn't stand a chance against three grown men . . . unless two of the men were nearly fifty and a little out of shape . . . and one of the two had been drinking all night. Tom would have to do most of the fighting, she realized, and one man against . . .

She looked back over to the car for an accurate count. Five boys against one man, a lush, an overweight maintenance man, and a woman stood a very good chance of inflicting a great deal of injury, she brooded. And what if they had weapons? Everyone and their uncle had a weapon these days.

"You need a ride, mama? I don't mind watchin' you walk, but you'd be a whole lot more comfortable in here with us. You can even sit on my lap," the spokesboy said, leaving no room to misinterpret his words.

She wanted to tell them to go home to their mothers, but the last time she'd heard, it was generally thought best to remain calm and try to ignore young people who liked to harass vulnerable, single woman.

But ignoring them wasn't easy, and neither was trying to appear calm. Her heart was racing and her palms were sweaty. Her heels began to click faster on the pavement.

"Hey, mama. We got party favors."

Click. Click. Click.

It wasn't until she heard one of them tell the driver to pull over that she began to run. There wasn't a hundred feet between her and the door to safety, but it seemed like forever before she was able to reach it and begin pounding on it with both fists.

No one came.

She glanced over her shoulder. Floodlights placed in the shrubbery to display the building's name showed three of the youths approaching her. They'd fanned out, blocking all escapes routes.

"Oh, Lord, help me," she muttered, frantic, still beating on the heavy metal doors.

"Take it easy, lady."

"Yeah. We just want some fun. What's a matter with you?"

"Can't you see there's nobody home there?"

She turned then, removing the strap of her purse from her shoulder. She threw it at them. Their faces were cast in the shadows, and she couldn't see them clearly—which was probably a blessing.

"There. Take it and go away!" she shouted, hoping they'd be pleased with the *Electra-Love* money for the date and would leave her alone.

Suddenly she was being moved forward, toward the boys, from behind. She pushed back, not wanting to get any closer to them.

"Move away, Sydney," she heard Tom say from the other side of the door, his voice strained as he pushed. The door opened wide, and he stood, battle ready, on the walkway beside her. "Go back inside," he said without looking at her, his gaze fixed on the three young toughs.

She stepped inside, but didn't let the door close completely. If they didn't disperse immediately, now that they knew she wasn't alone, Tom was going to need help. She quickly scanned the lobby and was dismayed to see that neither of the maintenance men was present.

"Party's over, boys. Get lost," Tom said. He sounded commanding and authoritative, much to his own amazement. Having a showdown with a street gang wasn't something he did on a regular basis, and if anyone was interested in hearing the truth, he was scared spitless.

The boys, on the other hand, laughed at him and made several obscene remarks about Sydney's character and his own ambitions for the evening. But Tom's voice—strangely unaffected by the situation—remained calm and unimpressed. "You've had your fun. Take off," he said.

"Who's going to make us? You?"

"If I have to." Had he really said that?

There were more crude remarks and a few taunts as all but one of the young men moved back toward the street and the waiting car.

"You don't scare me, man."

Tom remained silent.

"I can take you, man. And I can have your woman. I been up against old guys like you before. Easy." He was shaking his hands and shuffling his feet from side to side. Tom didn't move a muscle. A vision of Sydney having to face the young hoodlums alone took hold in his mind and tore at something in his chest. It didn't make him feel any braver, but he understood that anything that happened to him couldn't be nearly as bad as the mere thought of it happening to her.

When it became apparent to his friends that the young warrior with the raging hormones was spoiling for a fight, the two youths at the curb presented a united front and rejoined their companion, jeering at and taunting Tom.

"Tom, come inside," Sydney called through the opening in the door. "The door locks automatically."

"Call the cops, Sydney," he said, still incredibly composed.

She hesitated, afraid to let the door close and shut him out completely. When it occurred to her that the police would have to be called one way or another, and that the sooner they got there, the better, she let go of the press-bar on the door and ran over to the telephone. Her purse and her money were out on the sidewalk, so she ran across the lobby to dial out at the reception desk.

As she spoke into the receiver, only vaguely aware of the questions and her answers, she caught sight of movement outside the door. The supposedly well-placed floodlights weren't placed well enough for her to see everything that was happening.

A youth fell, and then another. The back of Tom's jacket appeared in the long window of the door with a loud resounding bang on the metal. Then another youth fell—or maybe the same one fell again, she couldn't tell. Then Tom's head hit the door with a thump, followed by a second thump, and she heard the loud rumbling of the car pulling away.

Realizing that the police operator now had enough information to initiate some action, she dropped the receiver and ran back to where Tom stood waiting, his back to the street, his head lowered against the door.

"Oh, Tom. Are you all right?" She opened the door and pulled him inside, taking time only to make sure the door was securely latched. "I'm so sorry. What happened out there? I couldn't see."

"I'll be fine. One of them threw a rock or something at me."

It was then that she noticed the blood trickling down the side of his face from a gash on his right temple.

"Blood." She identified the vital fluid as her stomach protested at the sight of it and bile gathered in the back of her throat. All color drained from her face.

"Sit down here," she said, guiding him to a chair

in the lobby. Fishing in her jacket pocket for a tissue to wipe away the blood, she said, "I am so sorry. I should have come back with you. I leave here late all the time, and that's never happened before. Of course, I have a space in the parking garage, but . . . oh, I'm so sorry. Does it hurt?"

"Yes. A little." And then as it occurred to him he smiled at her. "That's the first time I've ever been called upon to come to a lady's rescue and defend her honor. I've always wondered how I'd react in such a situation."

"You were very brave. Do you have a handkerchief? All I have is tissue, and it's sticking to your face." He gave her his clean, pressed white linen handkerchief, and she was gratified to see that it covered the blood completely. "How does it feel to be a hero?" she asked, hoping a little levity would quiet her stomach.

"It hurts."

"Were you scared?"

"I thought I was going to wet myself out there."

"Really? You acted as if you face jerks like that twice a week for the fun of it."

"I did, huh?" He took on a smug expression, rather proud of himself. And despite the nausea she felt, her heart melted, and she felt glad to be alive. If she hadn't begun falling in love with him before, she sure was now, she decided.

"We need some water to get you cleaned up. Are you dizzy? Can you make it to the men's room?"

"Sure." He got up without any difficulty. "Actually, I think the shock's wearing off. I don't feel all that bad, and it only hurts when I touch it."

"Can you take care of it yourself, or would you like some help?" she asked, all in favor of letting him tend his own wounds. She wasn't insensitive or ungrateful for all he'd done for her, but she was loath to add insult to injury by vomiting on his shoes.

"I think it's stopped bleeding," he said, removing the white handkerchief from his wound to look at it. "I can probably handle it my—"

The wound, the dried blood, and the vivid red and white contrast of his makeshift dressing were too much. Sydney pushed past him into the men's room and embraced the first commode she came to.

"Aw, Sydney," he said seconds later, his hand on her forehead, his voice full of sympathy. "You poor baby. You must have been even more afraid than I was out there. I'm sorry. I didn't even stop to think about how you must be feeling."

She shook her head. "No. It's blood. Can't stand it," she said, gasping.

He chuckled softly. "You could have told me."

"You were hurt."

"Not that bad," he said. She began to relax, totally unaware of the affectionate smile on his lips. "You all right now?" She nodded, and he left her to pull herself together while he cleaned himself up.

She sorely missed the mints she had in her purse as she stood to tuck her blouse back into her skirt and button her jacket, but the cool metal of the stall door felt wonderful on her brow as she stood wondering what she'd done to deserve the punishment her nerves were taking that night.

Suddenly Charlie the maintenance man burst in. "Now what in bloody blue hell is going on?" he shouted. "Aren't you two ever going home? There are cops outside looking for you. I can't be runnin' up and down the stairs all night, letting people in and out of the building for phone calls and such. I got work to do, and I'll never get done . . ."

He continued to complain as Tom and Sydney walked past him, out the door and down the hall to greet the police. One of them handed over her purse.

Sydney repeatedly insisted that Tom needed to be taken to an emergency room, but he stoically refused to go, saying that the gash on his temple looked worse than it felt and that he was sure it wouldn't need stitches.

They took turns telling the details of the incident and giving descriptions. The officers thought it extremely amusing that they were game-show contestants, but did manage to listen to their story with straight faces. Halfway through, the cab arrived.

"You might as well tell him to go," one of the police officers said, speaking of the cab driver. "You'll need to go downtown and go through the mug books if you want to press charges."

Tom and Sydney looked at each other. Did they want to spend the rest of their night together in a police station going over mug shots of hoodlums who would most likely never be caught? Did they want to waste their time and efforts on what boiled down to an assault for which the youths wouldn't receive nearly the penalty they deserved?

"Do we have to press charges? Couldn't you just file your report, and if the same group of boys are ever arrested, call us and let us testify then?" Sydney asked, wanting the boys punished, but also wanting the entire incident to be over so that she and Tom could go on with their date—such as it was.

"Filing charges now would help, ma'am. Even if you're called in to testify later, it would hold more weight if you pressed charges now. You have to go downtown to file a stolen vehicle report anyway . . ." He shrugged.

Tom turned to Sydney. "Why don't you take the cab and go home. You didn't get a good look at them, you got your purse back, and there's no sense in our both going downtown tonight."

The black hand-held radio in the second officer's fist was squawking and humming loudly.

"Looks as if you'll be needing that cab after all, folks. We have another call," the officer said. He gave them the name of a lieutenant who would help them file their charges, wished them good luck on what was left of their date, and left.

"This'll work out fine," Sydney commented a short while later as she walked out to the waiting cab with Tom. "We can stop by an emergency room and have someone look at your forehead before we go to the police station."

"You could still go home."

"I want to make sure you get some medical attention. You could have a fractured skull. We need to go someplace and have your head X-rayed."

"I have a better idea," he said, holding the cab door open for her. "Let's skip the hospital and get something to eat instead."

"We could do all three. Hospital, fast food, cops . . . great date, huh?"

He grinned. "Next time, I get to do the planning. Your dates can be rough on a guy."

"Next time?"

"Next time."

Their gazes met, and the temperature inside the cab rose considerably. There was a look in Tom's eyes that was becoming familiar to her. It made her head spin while her heart did cartwheels. It created the strangest scary-excited feeling in the pit of her stomach. It was like a joy ride, but with the option to get off any time she wanted to.

Sydney had never liked those rides. Ferris wheels and roller coasters were for crazy people who got a rush living dangerously to flout death or for young people who didn't know any better. Sydney had a deep aversion to death. She carried whole life insurance. She wasn't planning to die. Ever.

Still, she was enjoying the odd feeling of recklessness Tom inspired in her. It wasn't life-threatening, of course, but the potential for pain and anguish were just as real as the thrill and exhilaration.

"Where to?" the cab driver asked, watching them through the rearview mirror.

"Emergency room. Fast food." They answered at once without breaking eye contact. Tom smiled.

"It's fine," he said, referring to his wound, his voice a whisper as he studied her face intently. It was a face he never wanted to forget, one he never wanted to lose sight of, ever.

"I can still see it," she uttered, engrossed in her own perusal of his fine features.

"Is it making you sick again?"

"No." *Sick* was not a word she'd use to describe what she was feeling. "The streetlight isn't shining on it. I can't even see that half of your face right now."

"So it wouldn't make you sick if I kissed you?"

"Maybe we should try it and see."

"Meter's running," the cab driver reminded them impatiently from the front seat.

Tom waved him away from the curb as he sucked sensuously on Sydney's bottom lip and nibbled on her tongue. Lord, how could a kiss be so pleasing and fulfilling and make him feel so dissatisfied and unfinished?

"Fast food?"

He gave the cab driver a thumb's up sign, and then used his hand to pull Sydney closer, kissing her deeply.

Five

Horns blared. Rubber squealed on asphalt. Glass shattered. The last thing Sydney heard was the whine of metal bending, and then she felt excruciating pain.

"Sydney? Oh, dear Lord. Sydney?"

From what seemed like miles away, she heard Tom's voice. She could see him, her eyes were open. But everything was very unreal. Like a dream.

"Can you move? Try to sit up." She saw him reach out to her, and a flash of red-hot pain shot through her body when he touched her arm. "Dammit. We need an ambulance. Somebody call an ambulance!" he shouted.

But there were other people shouting too. She vaguely wondered if she should call the others' attention to the fact that Tom was trying to tell them something, but it was too much of an effort.

"Hold your arm. Here, like that. Good. Now try to sit up and see if you can get out of the car. Does your back hurt? Or your neck?"

"No," she said. Well, at least she thought she said

it. She shook her head to make sure he got his answer. It seemed very important to him. He was extremely agitated, and he looked . . . worried.

But worried was Sydney's forte. She worried better than anyone she knew. Why wasn't she worried? Perhaps there was more going on than she realized?

"Good. Just a little bit more," Tom was saying, his voice gentle and concerned. "Careful. There's glass all over out here."

"Glass?"

"Sydney? Look at me." She did. "We've been in an accident, Sydney. I think your arm's broken."

At first she didn't believe him. Then, and only because he appeared so earnest and distressed, she took a look around.

There on the other side of the car stood the cab driver and a man in jeans and a T-shirt, screaming and shouting at each other and waving their fists in the air. Traffic in the next lane had all but come to a halt as people drove by at a snail's pace, gawking and staring . . . at her! She lowered her gaze to what dimly resembled the back seat of the cab. The car's interior was mutilated into a hideous shape, she noted, and . . . it glimmered. How odd.

Upon closer examination, she discovered that it was zillions of tiny pieces of glass sparkling like stars. Why, she even had some in her lap.

The two men in the street didn't appear to be hurt. She gave Tom a quick once-over and then glanced past him to see where they were. She saw her office building. They were still parked in front of her office building!

"This is a nightmare. I feel like I'm in the Twilight Zone," she wailed. "Why doesn't it just fall on us and get it over with?"

"What?" Tom asked, a bit flustered with her tears and disjointed babble.

"The building! It's trying to kill us. We'll never get away from it."

"Sydney." He put his arm around her, careful not to touch her left arm, and led her away from the cab. He tried to give her his handkerchief. She took one look at the dried blood on it and cried harder. He pried her grip from her purse and looked inside for some tissue. Not finding any, he stood up, yanked the tail of his shirt from his pants, and ripped it.

"Here. Use this," he murmured close to her ear, as he sat beside her on the curb and put his arm around her again. She found the sympathy in his voice irritating.

"We could have been killed."

"But we weren't," he said, knowing she was still in shock and too concerned with her injury to pay much heed to what she was saying. "Does it hurt when you move your fingers?"

She wiped her eyes and blew her nose in the tail of Tom's shirt, marginally aware of the aching pain and stiffness in her left arm.

"I'm not ever going to die, you know," she said, sniffing. "I don't want to, and I won't let it happen."

"Good. I like your spirit. Can you lift your arm up?"

"Did you get hit in the head again?" she asked, looking at him as if she'd never seen him before. "Don't you know what's happening? We could have been killed. Three times tonight, we could have been killed."

"But we weren't," he insisted gently. "We're safe. We're not going to die. In fact, I don't think your arm is broken after all. We're safe *and* sound. We're fine." He started picking through hair like a mother monkey. "Looks as if you got a couple pieces of glass in your head here, but it's not too bad. More blood than damage."

"*What* is the matter with you?" she asked, her voice rising dangerously close to a hysterical level. "You got bent out of shape about your damn car, but when our lives are threatened you act as if it's the most common, ordinary thing in the world. I feel I should tell you, Tom, that your priorities are drastically out of order, and I have to tell you that it annoys the hell out of me."

He laughed.

"Don't you dare laugh at me!"

"I'm sorry," he said, although he couldn't bring himself to appear contrite. "Don't be angry. I—" he chuckled again, "I'm thrilled that we're still alive. I can't remember being happier about it."

"Well, you have a strange way of showing it. You act as if your whole life is just one accident after another. Like you're used to living this way," she said, even as she rejected the idea of his being jinxed. She didn't believe in that sort of thing.

"I have had a lot of experience with adversity," he said, sobering as he began to understand her true complaint. "I get paid to remain calm when those around me are devastated. I've had a lot of practice. I guess that's why I save my emotional outbursts for things that don't really matter much, like my car."

"You get paid to be calm?"

He nodded. "I stay relaxed and take care of everything when other people are . . . aren't up to it."

She frowned. He'd brushed his profession aside earlier, but perhaps she shouldn't have let it slip by so easily. What did he do? Control a nuclear reactor? Earthquake relief? Manufacture dynamite?

"I thought it would take us longer to get back to job talk, but now you've got me curious. What is it exactly that you do?" she asked, glancing away long enough to take in the arrival of a police car.

"Human services, isn't going to cut it anymore, huh?" He felt like a doomed man. Timing was usually a crucial point when it came to telling people about his life. It wasn't the sort of thing you could blurt out at cocktail parties or in casual conversation . . . or moments after a car accident.

"Nope." She was confused by his reaction. "It can't be all that bad. You already know that I have one of the world's most boring jobs, and if yours is to remain calm while everyone else gets crazy, there must be some excitement to it."

He hesitated, and then asked, "If your job's boring, why do you stay with it? You're bright and intelligent. You could do anything."

"I am pretty smart," she said, glad that he'd noticed. "And I have an aptitude for numbers. Economics and commerce make sense to me. I read tax codes the way most people read newspapers. It isn't exciting, but I do enjoy the problem solving it involves. Finding the errors, manipulating funds for tax breaks . . . things like that. I'm good at it. That's why I stay with it." She paused to make eye contact with him. "Now it's your turn. What do you do and why do you do it?"

He looked away and took a deep breath. When he returned his gaze to hers, he seemed to have distanced himself somehow, protected himself with a hidden shield.

"The worst part of my job is the reaction it gets from people outside the profession," he said, his voice quiet. There was a plea for understanding in his expression and something else she couldn't decipher. Her heart went out to him, though she couldn't help but wonder what could possibly be so horrible. Was he the state executioner?

"I never know if women are interested in me or the mysticism associated with what I do." He shook his head in confusion and laughed. "Frankly, I've never been able to get into the mystical end of it. I'm more concerned with the here and now. But I guess I can see where it might have an appeal to certain types of women. My ex-wife for one."

Sydney was beginning to get the creeps. His words weren't making sense. What was he? A psychic? An American guru? Voodoo priest?

"I really tried to understand that part of her, but it was just too weird," he said, his thoughts in the past. "I didn't even know about it until after the wedding, and then it just got worse and worse."

"What got worse and worse? What did she do? What do you do?"

"Ma'am?" They both jumped, surprised by the police officer standing over them. "The driver says you were injured. Do you need an ambulance?"

"Yes."

"No," Sydney said. "My arm was hurt, but I don't think it's broken. See, I can move it and everything."

"She needs to go to a hospital," Tom said firmly, scowling at her. "She can't lift it over her head."

"Well, if it's not serious, we can drop you off at Mercy when we're finished here," the officer said kindly, eyeing Tom's facial laceration. "You might want the gash on your head looked at, too, sir."

Tom touched his forehead gingerly, as if he'd forgotten all about the previous incident. He chuckled. "This didn't happen in the accident. We've . . ." He looked at Sydney. "We're having one hell of a night."

Against her will and for no clear reason, his comment struck her as ridiculously funny. Sydney began to laugh, and it felt wonderful. It wasn't a wild hysterical laugh. It was a good, sane laugh that came straight from her heart. It released the despair and the sense of danger and helped her give up her worries.

She laughed until there were tears in her eyes, and through the blur she looked at Tom and felt friendship and camaraderie. She sensed she could trust him, depend on him to bring light into the darkness and make the unbearable tolerable. She was drawn to his optimism and easy, lighthearted nature.

He was a stabilizing force in her life. And she wasn't so ignorant or infatuated with the man that she didn't know his actions were quite deliberate. She'd heard the panic and fear in his voice after the accident, when he thought she'd been injured. She'd felt the gentleness in his touch. She'd seen his strength and his capacity for anger and rage in dealing with abuse and cruelty. In his eyes she'd seen intimacy, warmth, and a giving nature.

No, the man was no fool, she decided, watching him talk with the policeman. He'd felt everything she had felt. The shock, the fear, the pain. But he'd put it aside to meet *her* needs.

"Did you see what happened?" the officer asked, the question addressed to either one or both of them.

Tom's eyes twinkled merrily, his lips twitching with restrained mirth. She frowned until she recalled what they'd been doing at the time the accident occurred. She burst into giggles once more.

"It happened very quickly," Tom told the man with a straight face, not unaware of or ungrateful for the timely delay in having to tell Sydney what he did for a living. He wasn't ashamed of what he did, mind you. But it was a delicate subject, and he preferred to explain it in his own way, in his own time. "We didn't see anything."

"Do you know if your driver turned to look behind him before attempting to merge with the traffic? Or did he just pull out?"

"I really couldn't say," Tom said, laughter quivering in his voice. "I . . . we were preoccupied at the time."

"Oh" was all the officer said, as his features took on a knowing expression. He glanced from Tom to Sydney and smiled. He cleared his throat loudly. "Well, in that case I guess I can run you two up to Mercy Hospital real quick and come back for my partner. It won't take two of us to direct traffic till the tow truck comes."

Sydney caught the word *hospital* and sobered immediately.

"No. That's not necessary. I don't need to go to the hospital," she said, a familiar feeling of panic rising up inside her and sticking in her throat. "Really."

"Are you nuts? Of course you need to go," Tom said, frowning at her. "If your arm's not broken, then your shoulder is. You can't lift your arm. You need help."

"I can lift it," she said unequivocally. She got it as high as her left breast before she whimpered with the pain.

"That's it. Let's go," he said, pulling cautiously

but unrelentingly on her right arm. "No. Don't say another word. You're going."

"But, Tom, I—"

"No. You're going. I'll tell you what," he said, as he nudged her into the back seat of the patrol car. "If you behave, I'll have someone put a bandage on my head, so you won't have to look at it anymore. How's that?"

He slammed the car door before she could answer, and walked around to get in on the other side. He wedged her weak arm between them, supporting it with one hand while his other arm slipped protectively across her shoulders.

"Comfortable?" he asked.

"No. Well, yes, this is comfortable, but *I'm* not comfortable," she said, feeling cold suddenly. She shivered, and he inched closer to her to keep her warm. She realized that he didn't understand, that he was misconstruing everything because she wasn't making her feelings clear to him. Finally, she blurted, "Tom. I can't go to the hospital."

"Why not?"

"I can't, that's all. I just can't." She was so terrified and embarrassed, she could hardly speak.

There was silence for a few seconds. The officer got into the car, checked to make sure all was well in the back seat, and then started talking into the hand microphone of his radio.

Tom bent his head to look into her face. "If it's money, don't worry. I can . . . ," he said in a low voice.

"No. I have money. I . . . It's . . ." She just couldn't say it.

"What? Tell me, Sydney." His voice was soft and reassuring. "You were gung ho for the hospital when you thought I needed attention. Why won't you get some for yourself?"

"I can't," she whispered. "I wasn't going in with you. I would have waited outside."

"Why?" When she couldn't answer, he guessed. "You don't like hospitals."

She shook her head and then nodded. "I send flowers. I don't go inside."

"Why, Sydney? Why don't you like hospitals? Have you ever been inside one?"

"No. Not even when my cousin Francine had her baby. I tried. I stood there and the doors opened and closed and opened and closed, but I couldn't go in."

"Is it the smell that bothers you?"

"Somebody told me once that they have a distinct odor, that if you were blindfolded, you'd know where you were by the smell. Is it really awful?"

"No. Not awful, just . . . sterile, but distinctively hospitallike," he said, agreeing with what she'd heard but still eager to pinpoint her fears. "Tell me specifically, what it is that bothers you about hospitals?"

"Everything. Everything about hospitals scares me. I don't even drive past them. Cemeteries either. If there's one on the way to wherever I'm going, I drive for blocks to avoid it. I can't stand the sight of them."

"Cemeteries? You're afraid of cemeteries too?"

"You think I'm stupid, don't you?"

"No. I don't think you're stupid. You're trembling. But let's deal with one thing at a time here. Why do hospitals scare you?"

Sydney hated this part. Thankfully, she hadn't had to tell many people about it. It was easy enough to cover with one excuse or another, and she managed to keep it her secret most of the time. She wasn't proud of it. It was embarrassing and shameful at times. But it was also something she couldn't explain and couldn't overcome.

"Why do hospitals scare you?" he asked again, gentle but persistent.

"People die in hospitals," she muttered in the tiniest of voices.

"I'm sorry. I couldn't hear you."

She took a deep breath and said it again in a louder voice.

"What?" He couldn't believe what he was hearing.

"People die in hospitals."

He moved forward on the seat so quickly that he nudged her shoulder, and she winced in pain. He turned and looked back at her in astonishment and skepticism, braced with one arm on the back of the seat.

"People *die* in hospitals? Is that what you said?" She nodded, watching his reaction from her heart. "People also get well in hospitals and go on to live their lives."

"I know. But I'm not afraid of living, I'm afraid of dying. It's called thanatophobia."

"What?"

"Thana-toe-phobia."

"Thanatophobia." He looked as if they'd just finished having sex and she'd told him she had a social disease.

"It's . . . it's an unexplainable fear of anything that has to do with death. Blood, hospitals, life-threatening situations . . . when I think about dying, I get a little crazy or throw up or sometimes my heart beats so fast, I pass out. I don't know why, I just do. I mean, I've never been traumatized or died and come back to life or anything like that. It's just the way I am."

"So. Anything that has to do with death . . . upsets you?"

"Well, yes, sort of," she said, wondering what he was thinking, wondering if she should explain it to him, wondering if it would make a difference, wondering . . . Suddenly the choice was out of her hands. She'd already started to speak.

"When my mother used to take me to the psychiatrist, when I was little, he said that my case was mild compared to some he'd seen. I guess that's because I don't faint when I see dead birds or flowers. I . . . I've never seen a dead person, but he said that my reaction would be more to the reminder of my own death than to the dead person's death, that I'm more afraid of dying than I am of death in general. He said it was good that I could talk about it when I had to, and that I could recognize it for what it is—an irrational fear. But . . . but he also said that there wasn't much that could be done about it. A certain amount of fear was natural and normal. I just have a little too much."

She sighed and went silent, feeling relief at having her secret out in the open between them, but still too unsure of his reaction to look at him, wary of seeing the disbelief and displeasure in his face.

He groaned and fell back into a sitting position beside her. His head came to rest on the back of the seat; his eyes were closed. One arm came up to cover his face, and he started to chuckle. He should have known that Sydney was too good to be true, that there'd be a monkey wrench in the works somewhere. Love at first sight and happily-ever-after rarely worked as smoothly as they did in the movies. He knew that. But thanatophobia?

"Are you laughing at me?" she asked, feeling

tears of humiliation welling in her eyes. It hurt to think that he might not be able to understand, that he might reject her for something she couldn't control. She'd thought better of him. She'd thought *much* better of him.

"No. I'd never laugh at you," he said. "I'm trying not to cry. I don't know how much more of this night I can take."

There was weary disappointment in his voice and manner, despite his words of reassurance. His disillusionment hurt too. She'd wanted him to like her.

"I won't say I'm sorry for something I can't control," she said, swallowing the lump in her throat as she wiped a stray tear from her cheek. Perhaps she should have warned him. Maybe part of his frustration was her fault. "But I am sorry I didn't tell you earlier. I didn't think . . ." The tears came unchecked.

"Whoa," he said, turning to her quickly. "You don't have one damn thing to apologize for, Sydney. Really. I wish I'd known sooner. I had no idea what you were going through, but you don't have to feel bad about any of it."

"You don't think it's disgusting, that I have an obsessive fear of dying? You don't think I'm weird or strange or being a baby about it?" she asked, grasping the lapel of his suit and blubbering against the front of his shirt. "Some people do, you know. And I wouldn't blame you if you did. I'm analytical and systematic. I'm too . . ." She searched her memory for Judy's word. ". . . linear to be irrational."

She felt his chest vibrate and heard the laughter in his voice when he said, "Well, I don't know that I'd describe you as linear, but I also wouldn't call you disgusting, weird, strange, or babylike—

although I do enjoy holding you as if you were one."

With a light touch to her chin he tenderly raised her face to his. He took the shirttail from her fingers and dabbed at the tears on her cheeks before he pressed a soft, caring kiss to her lips.

Sydney inspired a protective instinct in him that was gentle, warm, and fierce, and unlike anything he'd ever felt before. It wasn't chivalry or valor or as macho as the strong protecting the weak. It was more like what an animal would feel protecting its mate or its young. An innate reaction to anything threatening something vital to its own well-being. It was a new feeling for him, and he liked it.

"I think you're a beautiful, intelligent woman," he murmured against her lips, "with glass in your hair and a broken shoulder. I also think that you and I need to talk more about this later." He glanced through the front window as they approached the hospital's emergency room. "But right now, we need to figure out what we're going to do about getting you fixed up. What about a clinic?"

"In my head, they're the same as a hospital."

"Then we don't have a choice. You're going to have to trust me," he said, as the car stopped outside a large set of automatic doors.

"Oh, Tom. I don't know," she said, her trepidation clear. Tom got out of the car and bent to help her out. She couldn't move. Her gaze was glued to the big glass doors.

"Sydney, honey, trust me. I'll be with you the whole time, and I promise I won't let anything bad happen to you. I'll talk you through everything." He studied her fearful expression and waited for his words to settle into her mind. "Trust me to take care of you, can you do that? Can you trust me?"

She looked at him then, appearing vague and disoriented, as if trust were a new concept for her. The portico light delineated his features. They were strong and confident. Tall and sturdy, built to withstand the forces of the world around him, he appeared to be a man she could rely on. She knew he was a man she could depend on to cope and function when she could not. But was he a man she could trust with her heart, her dignity, and her pride?

"You do trust me, don't you?" he asked, a troubled note in his inflection when she took too long in answering.

"Yes." She didn't sound as sure as she felt. She did trust him, but she didn't know if he had a real idea of what he was getting himself into. "But what if I . . . do something embarrassing? What if my nose starts to bleed or I pass out or I start to scream? What if I punch someone or start tearing my hair out and—"

"You're not going to do any of those things. I promise. Come on, get out." He took her right hand, and when she was safely out of the vehicle, he thanked the police officer and then turned her toward the hospital entrance.

"Hold on to my hand as tightly as you want to," he said, walking slowly toward the doors. "Don't hear anything but my voice. Don't think about anything except what I'm telling you." The doors opened like a sideways set of jaws. "Does your arm hurt?"

"My arm?" There were people on the other side of the door. Not nurses or doctors, she judged, since they were wearing street clothes and seated in small groups, impatiently waiting. "What's the matter with these people?" she whispered, turning her back on them to face the exit.

Tom caught her and bent his knees to look into her face.

"These people are just like you. They're hurt or sick and they're here to get help. They're waiting to see a doctor. It's the same as going to the doctor's office. You sit and wait your turn. You've done that before, haven't you?"

She lowered her eyes and hung her head. "A long time ago," she murmured, recalling the past with terror and mortification. "But my mother used to call ahead to warn them. We didn't have to wait and I . . . I didn't behave very well."

"How long ago was that?"

She shrugged.

"Sweetheart, you need help." She looked up quickly to see if he was being condescending, but saw only his concern. "You need checkups," he said. "What do you do when you're sick?"

Again she shrugged and looked away. She knew most people saw a doctor on a regular basis and for every little sniffle they contracted. It was the American way. She felt like a traitor. "I wait for it to go away."

He was ready to argue the point, but he didn't. "Okay. We can talk about this later too," he said. "The first thing we do is go over to that desk there and tell them we want to see a doctor. Do you have insurance?"

"Yes."

"They must love you. Come on." He led her over to an enclosed reception area, more dragging than leading actually, and while she stood silently by, he did all the talking.

"Do you have an insurance card?" he asked. "Or has it turned to dust from neglect?"

"Is this the smell you were talking about? Does it always smell like this?"

He nodded. "Pretty much. You all right?"

No. She wasn't all right. He sounded as if he were talking from the inside of a fishbowl. Her heart was racing, and she felt a little light-headed. And the people who moved in slow motion around her were staring rudely at her—as if she were a freak in a sideshow. None of them appeared about to die, but perhaps this was why they were staring at her. Maybe they could see that she was dying. Maybe they all knew. Maybe they could feel it too.

She looked at Tom and nodded. "I'm fine," she said bravely, refusing to make a scene. Tom was going to have enough to deal with when she slipped silently into oblivion—or to whatever existed or didn't exist beyond life. In her mind she heard him explaining her death.

"*She was kicking and screaming and clawing at her face one minute and dead the next. I've never seen anything like it. Sydney was one weird chick, if you ask me.*"

"Sure? You're pale. Do you want to sit down?"

"Are you going to sit down?" she asked, gripping his hand as she would a lifeline.

"In a second," he said. He took up the purse that dangled from her shoulder, pulled out the brown leather wallet, and picked through it with one hand until he found her insurance card, which he gave to the receptionist. "We're going to have a bunch of questions to answer here. Are you up to it?"

"Sure."

He took a clipboard with a few sheets of paper attached from the receptionist and led Sydney by the hand to sit in a secluded corner of the room.

Six

"This is going to be great," Tom said, smiling his enthusiasm as he settled into the chair beside her in the waiting room.

The people around them were solemnly quiet, adding fuel to Sydney's *dis*quiet. If a hospital was a place of healing and miracles, why wasn't anyone smiling? she wondered. Except Tom, of course. But even his smile was marred by the anxious concern in his eyes.

"Now I'll know you inside out," he said. "I should have started bringing my dates here years ago." He paused. "Not funny, huh? Well, you'll get a charge out of these questions—one way or another. Is Sydney Wiesman your full name?"

"Isadora."

"Sydney Isadora Wiesman is your full name?" She nodded, hardly noticing the humor in his voice as she eyed the people seated in front of them, waiting for one or more of them to fall over dead. "No doubt about it now," she heard him saying. "We have to go out again. I want you to tell me all about your mother."

"Why?"

He looked down at the clipboard and the name he'd written on it and shook his head. "Forget it. How old are you? And don't lie."

The board on his lap, he was writing with one hand—while the fingers of the other one turned white under the pressure of her grip. He continued to ask numerous questions, some of which were quite embarrassing, considering she hadn't known him eight hours.

Tom didn't act as if he had the slightest compunction in asking personal questions such as whether or not she had regular bowel movements or when her last menses had occurred and what she used for birth control. As a matter of fact, he appeared to be having a rather good time of it—or so it seemed from the comments he made.

And if the truth were known, there were several occasions she wanted to laugh with him but couldn't. It was like listening to a comedian while on her way to the gallows. No matter how funny or clever the jokes, she couldn't laugh.

His efforts weren't in vain, however. He was trying so very hard to keep her distracted and her spirits up, and for that alone she was grateful and etched his name in her heart for all time.

They were halfway through a long, gruesome list of gastric anomalies—many of which she was sure she was developing as they spoke—when the big doors opened wide again to admit a young woman with a baby in her arms.

Sydney didn't see each of them individually, she saw one complete picture—distraught mother holding a quiet, listless child. She was struck by the stillness of the infant.

"Oh, no," she said with a gasp, thinking the worst. "Not a baby."

She loved children. They were always so active and busy. They had such zest for life, they were the last ones she'd ever associated with death. Somehow a child's death was worse than the thought of her own demise.

"What?" Tom asked, looking up to see the horror in her face and swiftly following her stare to the young mother and child. He was quick to catch on. "Hang on now, Sydney. We don't have all the facts yet. Babies get sick, too, but it doesn't mean they die. It's late at night, and their pediatrician's office is closed. It could be something as simple as a bad cough."

"Why doesn't it move?"

"It is moving. Look. It's sucking its thumb and looking around. It's late," he repeated. "It's probably sleepy."

Upon closer examination she found his words to be true. The baby wasn't dead yet, but its skin was unusually red and it had a glazed expression in its eyes. She continued to watch the child closely and answered the rest of Tom's questionnaire in monosyllables.

He finished just as the mother turned away from the receptionist and started searching for a place to sit.

"I'm going to take these back to the desk now. You stay put," he said, scanning her face for signs of mental distress.

"Tom. Thank you. You're being very kind about all this," she said, self-conscious, wanting him to know how she felt in case there wouldn't be another chance to tell him. "You're a very patient man."

"Not always, but I'm glad you think so." He smiled at her.

She was amazed for a second or two that she

hadn't noticed how long his dark lashes were. And his eyes were so blue. She wondered if he'd noticed that people were being called away, disappearing behind a set of metal doors and not coming back.

"Will you be okay here for a minute?" he asked.

"Yes," she said automatically, not knowing if she would be or not, as she watched the woman with the child seat herself two chairs away.

The woman literally had her hands full. With the baby in her arms, a diaper bag, her purse, and the clipboard, she seemed uncertain as to which to set down first.

"Is your baby terribly ill?"

The woman glanced up in surprise at Sydney's question.

"I'm sorry. It's none of my business," Sydney said, fixing her stare on her hands as they tied knots in the tail of Tom's shirt.

"Oh, that's okay. I don't mind," the young woman said cordially. "To tell you the truth, he probably isn't ill at all. I panic too easily."

"You do?" Sydney was impressed. It was a comfort to know that she wasn't the only person losing her mind.

"Sure. The last time I brought him here in the middle of the night with a fever, he was teething. Boy, did I feel stupid. I'd even given him some Tylenol at home, and by the time we got here, it'd kicked in and his fever was gone. I'm sure they all thought I was crazy, but I don't care. I have two other children, but I only have one Andrew. Isn't that right, pal?" she asked the baby, tapping his nose with the tip of her finger, making him smile at her around his thumb. "And I was just as crazy with the other two, wasn't I? Yes, I was."

"He's awfully red," she said, sounding concerned enough that the woman didn't take offense.

"It's the fever. I gave him medicine at home, but it doesn't look as if he's going to make a liar out of me this time. Feel how hot he is."

Sydney glanced from mother to child and back again, startled by the invitation. Still, she couldn't think of a reason not to touch the child, so she stood up and walked closer to them. Tentatively, she pressed the back of her hand to the baby's overly rosy cheek. He was the hottest human she'd ever touched. She'd had sunburns that were cooler than Andrew. The phenomenon was quite disconcerting.

"He's so hot," she murmured.

"Scary, huh?" the woman said, although she wasn't giving the proper impression of a frightened mother as she set her purse and diaper bag on the seat beside her. Frankly, Sydney thought her a master of understatement. The heat emanating from Andrew was more than scary.

She watched the woman fumble with the clipboard and the baby, trying to find a free hand. "I could fill that out for you, if . . . if you tell me what to write," Sydney said.

They were both astonished by her offer. She had no idea why she'd tendered her services, except maybe for Andrew. If Tom was right, and she was trusting with all her might and every frazzled nerve in her body that he was, people often got well in hospitals and were released. At that moment, she wanted more than anything else to see that happen for Andrew.

His mother handed the board and pencil to Sydney and settled back to cuddle him in her arms. She viewed Sydney with a kind but speculative eye, and when she'd answered all the questions, she nodded at Tom and asked, "Is that your, ah, friend? You're not wearing a ring, so I assume you're not married."

She looked over her shoulder at Tom and gave the question some thought. She smiled at him and watched his expression light up as he repaid her the favor.

"Yes. He's my friend."

"I thought so. You two look as if you were in the same wreck. Are you in a lot of pain?" She lowered her eyes to Sydney's left arm, held protectively close to her chest.

"Less than when it first happened," she said, wondering exactly how much like an accident victim she looked. She hadn't thought about her appearance in hours and could only dimly recall the pleasure she'd known earlier at being dressed to perfection for her big game-show date. "I guess I'm lucky that Andrew hasn't screamed at me. I must look a fright."

She felt even luckier that Tom hadn't screamed yet.

When he stood and took the clipboard from her hand and walked it to the reception desk for them, the woman quickly leaned over Andrew and whispered, "He's been watching you . . . with *that* expression in his eyes. And he's *sooo* cute. You'd better nail him down before he gets away."

She nodded absently as she watched Tom returning to his seat. He was someone special, she decided, aware of a deep, penetrating warmth surging through her. Did she know anyone as kind or thoughtful as Tom? Had she ever met another man as understanding or patient with her faults as Tom? Certainly his wit and his broad base of knowledge set him apart from her other dates. There wasn't a doubt in her mind that he had the sexiest blue eyes she'd ever seen. Nor had anyone ever excited her emotions and made her feel so much *herself* before.

Sydney sent the young mother a woman-to-woman grin as she stood to go back to her place beside Tom. He took her right hand and gave it a gentle squeeze.

"Sydney Wiesman?" A nurse stepped out from behind the metal doors and called again. "Sydney Wiesman?"

"Here," Tom said, standing to go back to the treatment rooms with her.

The nurse took one look at Tom and grinned from ear to ear.

"Come on, Sydney. We can do this together," he said, his eyes bright with confidence.

"You're next," the nurse said, glancing at Sydney with a much smaller smile.

"Ah . . . actually, I think this lady and her baby were here before us," she said. True, her heart was pounding with fear, but she would have taken her turn without protest if Andrew hadn't arrived—she'd prepared herself for that eventuality when Tom hadn't shown any signs of backing away from the idea that she needed medical attention. But Andrew was a baby. She was sure she could hold out longer against the clutches of death than he could. "Maybe you should help them first."

The nurse made an impatient gesture and muttered something Sydney couldn't hear, but she flipped her clipboard back onto the counter and searched through the others until she finally found Andrew's.

"Andrew Reilly," she called.

"Thank you," the young woman said, gathering up Andrew and her paraphernalia and standing to follow the nurse. "This usually takes hours."

Sydney watched as they disappeared through the doors, and then turned to Tom to find him watching her.

"What? Why are you looking at me like that?" she asked, pink cheeked from the pleasure and appreciation she saw in his eyes.

"Will you marry me?" It was the third time he'd asked her that night, and the third time he'd caught her off guard.

"What?"

"Beautiful, bright, *and* compassionate. I don't think I can live without you."

She smiled in spite of herself. Marriage was no joking matter at this point in their relationship.

"That was a nice thing you did," he whispered in her ear, tickling the sensitive skin below the lobe.

"How do you know I wasn't just being a chicken? Making that poor baby go before me, so I could put it off a little longer?"

"Because I saw the way you were looking at him," he said, billowing the loose hairs that curled along her cheekbone. "I liked it. And if you marry me, you could look at our babies that way anytime you wanted to."

"Will you stop?" she said, feeling immensely uncomfortable, though not so much so that she couldn't enjoy the picture he was painting for her.

"Why? I think it's a great idea. We could go straight from here to the airport and catch the first flight to Vegas. We'd have to return Rex Swann's money, though, because I couldn't take the two-week waiting period to start our honeymoon."

"Do you know we haven't spent a dime of the money yet?" she asked, aware that he was teasing her, trying desperately to change the subject.

"We could use it on the honeymoon suite at the Sands."

"Sydney Wiesman?" With an odd mixture of relief and disappointment, she looked over at the nurse who had called out her name. "Is it your turn yet?"

Aside from a small group of people waiting for a man who'd already gone back to be treated and a man with a mop and bucket from housekeeping, Sydney and Tom were the only people left in the room.

"I guess so," she said, swallowing hard. Her stomach shifted into her throat. She felt a flash of heat engulf her body. It made her palms sweat and her skin feel clammy all over. She wondered if Andrew's fever made him sick to his stomach too.

"It's okay, Sydney," she heard Tom say as if from miles away. He took her arm and helped her to stand. "I'll be right there with you. I won't leave you for a second."

"Are you a relative?" the nurse asked Tom when they'd reached the metal doors.

"I'm her husband, and she's not feeling herself. Rough night. I think I should stay with her," he said, without the slightest quiver of a hesitation.

Sydney looked at him, but his quelling grimace kept her from denying his words.

The nurse shrugged and led them into a hallway exactly like the one Sydney had pictured in her mind. There were stretchers lining the walls, some occupied, some not. There was—stuff—all over, medical things such as wheelchairs, plastic canisters, blue and white boxes of gauze, tape, syringes, and tubes; color-coded paper, charts, coffee mugs, and an endless array of machines, gadgets, and doohickeys. A blackness closed in around Sydney, cutting off much of her view. She seemed to be looking at everything through a tunnel.

"Sydney?" It was Tom's voice again. "She wants you to get up on this stretcher here." She could see his hand patting it. "You need to take off your jacket and top and put on this gown."

That was when time and events began to blur and run together. Hands and faces came and went, but the only ones she recognized were Tom's. There was no pain, no fear. She existed in a vacuum. Tom would bend over her and speak, but she wasn't sure if she answered. She traveled as if on air, lights coming and going at irregular intervals. And then, abruptly, she was standing outside the big glass doors with a bright blue sling on her arm, cold in the early light of dawn.

"Here, this'll keep you warm till the cab comes," Tom was saying, as he wrapped his navy blue sport jacket around her shoulders. The jacket still retained his body heat, numbing the chill almost immediately. "I could tell you were nervous from the look in your eyes, but no one else saw it, I'm sure. I'm so proud of you. You acted as if the whole thing was a lark. They were in stitches. We all were, actually." He staged a scolding frown. "And you said you'd used up all your good jokes in the elevator."

"I did?"

"When you started in with a bigamist being an Italian fog and Camelot being a place to park camels, I was worried. But obviously you were just warming up. I laughed so hard, my face hurt." His heart had hurt too. He'd never been prouder of anyone in his life.

"You did?"

"Damn right. It was the best time I've ever had in a hospital."

"Me too." It was also the only time she'd ever been in a hospital, she thought, disgruntled. It annoyed her that the one time in her life when she was the life of the party would also be the one time her memory failed her. It didn't seem fair, considering the anguish she'd put herself through earlier.

He grinned at her and gave her an affectionate but careful squeeze. "I guess it's true that everyone responds to fear in a different way. I work on an ulcer, and you get hilarious."

"You have ulcers?" she asked, knowing that he felt and reacted to more things than he let himself show.

"Not yet. But I was working pretty hard on one back in the waiting room. I didn't know what you'd do, or whether or not I should have forced you to go in there. I was so afraid that I'd made the wrong decision and that I might be causing you some serious damage—mentally, I mean. I thought *I* was going to die."

In his face she saw the remnants of his fear and strife—and the great tenderness he had for her.

"You were wonderful," she said, sure that he had been from his initial behavior—and from his manner throughout the entire disaster of an evening.

"You *are* wonderful," he said, turning her slightly for better aim as his mouth came to rest over hers. He was a man with deep feelings and a great need. He let his kiss tell her that they were for her.

She returned his passion ounce for ounce. She took and treasured what he offered her and gave back in kind. She reveled in a sense of having found her niche, of having the jagged, irregular edges of her life smoothed and contoured, of fitting pieces of who she was together and making herself whole.

She aligned her body against his, and he tightened his embrace. His hands worked their way down her back to her buttocks, where he held her firm, impressing his desire against the wild ache near the juncture of her legs. She grew languid with longing and raised both arms to cling to him, wincing at the pain in her left shoulder.

"I'm sorry," he said, distressed that he'd hurt her.

"It wasn't your fault," she said, feeling her arm and noting for the first time that it hadn't been put in a cast.

"We were lucky that it wasn't broken. A couple of weeks in the sling, and you'll be as good as new," he said. And then, inspecting the top of her head, he added, "Course, your hair might be another story."

"What?" she exclaimed, her right hand flying to explore the damage.

"Well, they washed all the blood out, so you don't look as if you spent the night with Freddy Krueger anymore. But the antiseptic they used turned the whole top of your head orange. You look like a punk rocker." He grinned.

"Swell," she said, thankful that her light-colored hair was short and grew quickly, wondering what they would say at the office when she showed up wearing a hat—and wore it all day long.

"Are you Mr. Ghorman?" They both turned at the sound of the voice. The receptionist who had taken all the information from them earlier stood in the doorway rubbing her arms to ward off the early morning chill.

"Yes?" he called back, perplexed.

"There's a police officer by the name of Bobby Trent on the phone. He says he dropped the two of you off here earlier? He'd like to talk to you," she said.

Sydney groaned. What now? she wondered.

"I'll be right there." His gaze swept the vicinity

quickly. "We'd better not push our luck," he said, grinning. "I can watch you through the window, and I shouldn't be long. You don't need to go back inside if you don't want to."

"Good. I'll wait for you here. Do you suppose this has something to do with the accident?"

He shrugged and began to walk away. "He might need to know how badly you were injured for his report. I'll be right back."

Sydney turned to the sunrise as the doors swished opened and closed behind her. There was something about a sunrise that inspired hope and renewed the spirit. It had an air of fresh starts and new beginnings. She was glad to see another day dawn, feeling positive that the night had come to an end.

Frankly, it was becoming harder and harder to find the good in all that had transpired. Aside from meeting Tom, of course. In ten or fifteen years, she was sure she'd laugh at the entire episode. But at the moment, she wanted it to be over, a part of her past, a nebulous memory. All of it, except for Tom.

It didn't seem fair to Sydney that her happy thoughts of Tom were marred in the recollection of nearly every moment they'd spent together. Although it did seem to be the way of things, that good and bad came together. She thought of all the days when nothing too disastrous happened but nothing very exciting occurred either, and compared them to the ups and downs of the night she'd just lived through.

If the Fates ruled destiny, they were three of the most poorly organized women ever created, Sydney decided with great disdain. If it were up to her, there would be good times and then bad times with periods in between in which to adjust. She would have spent a horrible night with a CPA date, adjusted, and spent a romantic night with Tom . . . on his boat, she decided firmly.

Of course, if one believed in a person's free will to choose his or her own destiny, that would mean that Sydney had made some pretty rotten choices in the past few hours.

"Don't look so worried," Tom said, returning to her side. "It's good news this time."

"No. It can't be," she said in jest, smiling at him.

"Truly. Honest." He crossed his heart with one finger. "The cops have my car."

"They found it? Where?"

"A couple of blocks from where I'd left it. They think some kids took it for a joyride, but didn't want to get caught and tried to return it. He said a taillight was broken, but other than that it was in great shape," he said, beaming. "The last time, they never did find the car. It just disappeared off the face of the earth."

"See. I knew it," she said, delighted. "It's a new day and our luck is changing."

"It didn't have anywhere to go but up." He curved his arm around her waist as he saw the cab they'd been waiting for pull into the hospital driveway. "Tell me what you need the most. Food? Or to go straight home to bed?"

Ten minutes before she would have answered that she needed to go to bed—for about two weeks. But with their new good fortune, she felt her energy and optimism returning to near normal.

"What I need most is another kiss," she said, letting her eyes and her smile invite him to perform the honors. He didn't hesitate to accept. He gave her a wild, wonderful kiss that made her stagger a bit when he pulled away.

He held her at arm's length and looked as if he were bursting with things to tell her. Instead, he made a frustrated growling noise and opened the door of the cab.

"We need to find a quiet place and have a long talk, Sydney," he said, as she got into the back seat of the cab. A real long talk, he added to himself. "As soon as possible."

"Okay," she said, eager to hear what was on his mind. "How's this for a plan? We go to a convenience store, run in and buy coffee and something sticky and full of sugar to eat on the way to pick up your car, and then we go someplace quiet and talk over a huge breakfast." She hesitated briefly. "Unless you meant as soon as possible another day. If you're tired, we could talk some other time. I could go either way."

"No. It's important. Breakfast sounds fine." He lowered his eyes and toyed with the single button on her jacket. "And then do we go home to bed?" he added.

He raised his gaze back to hers. Her eyes were shining with amusement, a little bit of a challenge, and a whole lot of ambition.

Very deliberately she twisted one of the buttons on the front of *his* shirt, taking her time before she answered.

"Maybe."

"That's better than a flat-out no," he said, suddenly invigorated. He leaned over the front seat, gave the cab driver directions, and sat back beside her with a satisfied smile. They both turned to gaze out the rear window as the cab pulled away from the curb. They sighed their relief together and then laughed themselves silly.

Seven

They had to ride across town to the police impound parking lot, but they passed the time feasting on jelly doughnuts and coffee, which they shared with the driver, and telling legendary tales of their past. They'd both had grandfathers with a love for water sports from whom they'd inherited their own passions. She couldn't bear fishing but she loved sailing, while Tom enjoyed both immensely.

So often it struck her that they suited each other perfectly. Not like a hand in a glove, which was too perfect. But more like two pieces of a puzzle, where the connection between them was asymmetric and uneven. She had a tendency to fly off the handle and react to her emotions, while Tom was quick to think and saved his reactions until the crisis was over. Each of their personalities integrated with and compensated for the other's, and the bond between them merged in a unique but satisfactory fashion.

Standing beside Tom's classic white Lincoln in a huge lot while he answered a hundred questions and signed almost as many forms, Sydney pondered the possibilities of a future with Tom.

She conjured up pictures of a beautiful beach house with a white picket fence around the deck. There were children in sparkling white swimsuits playing in the surf. She saw herself waving to them fondly, dressed in a bright white sundress and a white lace broad-brim hat, with Tom in a white summer suit standing beside her looking content and well fed. Wouldn't life be grand? she mused with a deep, wistful sigh.

"I didn't have to go through that much trouble to buy the damned thing," Tom said, his key in the door of the passenger's side. It was daylight. He'd spent ten hours with her, and he still hadn't told her what he did for a living. He needed to tell her about his life, about who and what he was, but for the life of him, he didn't know how—and it was beginning to eat at his nerves. "Lord, you'd think it was my fault it was stolen."

She floated, half-dreaming, around the front of the car to get in as he held the door open for her. The force with which he slammed the car door had little effect on the sound it caused inside the well-built car, but it was enough to bring Sydney's head out of the clouds and make her take notice.

Tom was distracted and frustrated when he got in beside her.

"What's wrong, Tom?" she asked in a soft voice, leery of his anger, unsure of how to respond to it. She watched as he opened his mouth to tell her, thought better of it, and pressed his lips tightly closed. His body drooped, he sighed heavily, giving her a weary smile.

"I think I'm getting tired," he said, but she didn't believe him. The agitation was gone from his voice, but whatever caused it was not. She could see it in his eyes, though she couldn't identify it.

It embodied a mixture of emotions ranging from dread to resignation to fear and despair. He lowered his eyelids as if to conceal the conflict within him and went to great pains not to look directly at her while he started the car and maneuvered it out of the lot.

He had to tell her. He knew that. But after all she'd been through, how was he going to explain his life to her without sending her away screaming? Why did life always have to be so complicated? he wondered angrily.

He paused. Pondering life's complexities wasn't going to get him what he wanted. He knew that too. His energies would be better served if he could concentrate on a solution, he resolved. And there was a solution. There had to be. There was something about Sydney that made his heart smile. She was a counterbalance to the rest of his life. Even her phobic fear of dying had a way of certifying his convictions that life was precious—too precious not to do all the things you wanted to do, not see all the things you wanted to see, or not to be with the person you loved.

He'd made his share of mistakes. He'd done things and then wished he hadn't, seen things that were better left unseen. But nothing in all his life had felt as right or as natural to him as being with Sydney.

Timing. It was always a matter of timing, he decided. Telling her at just the right time with just the right words. Problem was, he ruminated, their timing seemed to be out of sync with the rest of the universe.

She remained silent as well, pondering the sudden tension between them and fighting the urge to ask questions. It wasn't polite to pry, but that was exactly what she wanted to do. His abrupt, undefined change in demeanor was bewildering, and it hurt. She'd trusted him and confided her darkest secret to him, yet he didn't seem to trust her.

He'd kept his best foot forward all night, showing her only his finest side. His intellect, wit, confidence, enthusiasm . . . the giving side of himself. Except for an occasional display of understandable anger, he'd hidden all his weaknesses. But it wasn't anger she'd glimpsed in his expression. It was something else, something that made him feel uncertain and troubled. It was something he didn't think she could understand, something he thought was beyond her empathy and compassion. It was something he was afraid to tell her.

"Do you know what time it is?" he asked, breaking the silence awkwardly, trying to sound incredulous.

"No." She was more curious as to what he was hiding from her, but knew she couldn't force him to believe in her. Still, maybe with time . . .

"Six-fifteen. What respectable restaurant serves breakfast at this hour? We can't even get an Egg McMuffin yet."

"Who'd serve us anyway? I look like I've been in a wreck and you look—" she glanced down at the shirttail hanging out from under his jacket, "shredded. We'd look very strange, even at McDonald's."

He took stock of the blood on their clothes and the mass of wrinkles that had at one time been their carefully chosen first-date duds and gave her a wry smile.

"You're a slob," he said, teasing her.

"Ha. This from a man who looks like he went to college and majored in hog calling?"

He gasped dramatically. "That from a woman

who'd wear a pink suit that clashes with her orange hair?"

"Oh yeah? Well, at least I . . . Oh, Tom, your eye."

He glanced at the light green discoloration under his left eye in the rearview mirror. "Hey, I like the way this green sets off the black and blue around my cut, don't you?" he asked.

"Sure. I clash, but you're color-coordinated. Typical male," she said, brushing him off lightheartedly.

"There's nothing typical about me, and you know it. I happen to be—" he broke off as he glanced up into the rearview mirror again. "Aw, hell! Now what?"

Sydney turned and saw red and blue lights flashing.

"The registration's in there," he said, indicating the glove compartment under the dash. There was a distinct edge to his voice as he tried to control his irritation.

He pulled over to the side of the road, turned off the engine, and rolled down his window in a jerky, agitated motion. She handed him the registration card and glanced back to see that the police car had pulled up behind them.

"Were we speeding?" she asked.

"No."

"The taillight," she said, feeling absolutely brilliant. "It's broken, remember? Maybe he wants to tell you about it."

He nodded, but he was afraid to be too hopeful. The night had put a severe strain on his power to be optimistic.

They heard footsteps approaching the car. Tom turned his head to greet the officer. He stuck his nose into the barrel of one ugly, lethal-looking gun.

Out of reflex more than true feeling, he muttered an oath in shock and surprise and didn't move a muscle. He should have been expecting this, he thought fatalistically.

Sydney's door flew open in that same moment, and she twisted in her seat to see the gun's twin aimed straight at her chest. She began to pray. "Oh, dear Lord."

"Keep your hands in sight," the policeman told Tom, his voice loud and full of authority. With his weapon in Tom's face, he lowered one hand to release the latch on the car door, but he didn't open it. "Get out."

Using his knee and foot, Tom pushed the door wide and got out.

"Assume the position," the officer barked.

"Now you," Sydney's officer said in much the same tone. "Keep your hands visible at all times."

She swung her legs to the ground and bent her head to stand, her right hand in the air. She turned to face Tom across the roof of the car with a thousand questions in her eyes. Her palms were damp, and there was a crushing tightness in her chest. It was her immediate assumption that she was going to spend the rest of her life in prison for . . . Lord, what *had* they done? it occurred to her to wonder.

"Can you tell us what this is all about, officer?" Tom asked in a cautious and overly civil voice, as the man ran his hands up and down his body. "Obviously this isn't a routine traffic violation."

"Shut up."

"Listen. We have a right to know why you pulled us over." A wave of pure pain washed into his features as Sydney turned and glared at the man groping her from behind. He couldn't hide his emotions any longer. "I demand to know what this is all about."

She was confused and terrified. She trembled as she felt the cold steel of handcuffs being snapped tightly around her wrists in front of her. She was hot and then cold. It was hard to take a complete breath. What was happening? Her mind was so muddled, she couldn't grasp a clear thought.

"Save it for the front desk, pal," the policeman said, clicking Tom's handcuffs into place from behind. He held the gun on Tom again as he bent to remove the keys from the ignition. "The only demand you'd better be making is the one to call your lawyer."

"But we haven't done anything to need a lawyer for."

"That's original." The man's attitude was thick with sarcasm. "You got any idea how many times I've heard that before?"

He walked past Tom to the trunk of the car. Sydney's officer backed away from her in the same direction. They unlocked the lid and raised it into the air, before pulling open the false bottom of the trunk to expose the cargo area underneath.

"I suppose you have no idea where any of this came from, either?" the first officer said, speaking as if he wouldn't believe a single word that came from Tom's mouth.

Slowly, Tom walked to the back of his car. Curious, even in her fear, Sydney did the same. They both stared, open-mouthed at two dirty off-white pillow cases from which had spilled an array of paper money, watches, rings, various types of other jewelry, and a single silver candlestick.

"Oh, tell me this isn't happening," Sydney muttered. She looked at Tom, who stood with his head lowered and his eyes closed as if he were praying for it to be a hallucination.

"Look," he said, feeling compelled to attempt an explanation, though he could feel the last threads of his patience unraveling and growing thin. "You've got it all wrong. This is an incredible misunderstanding, officer. My car was stolen last night. I just drove it off the impound lot."

"Save it for the judge, pal. You have the right to remain silent, so use it. You also have the right. . . ." He continued to Mirandize Tom while his partner returned to their vehicle to use the radio. When the officer began to recite Sydney's rights, Tom stopped him.

"Wait a second," he broke in. "The car belongs to me. She's not involved."

The officer looked back at her and asked, "Do you know that man?"

"Yes."

"Were you in his vehicle against your will?"

"No."

"Then you have the right to remain silent . . ."

"Look at her," he shouted angrily. "She's hurt. How could she rob a pawn shop with one arm in a sling? It's my car. I'll take full responsibility. Call her a cab and let her go home."

"Look, pal—"

"I'm not your pal." Tom wanted that made perfectly clear.

"You stand there and keep your mouth shut and let me read the lady her rights. Then we'll run you in, and you can do all your explaining to the detective assigned to the case," the officer said in no uncertain terms.

Two hours later, they were sitting in a near empty room at the police station, apprehensive, exhausted, and exasperated.

Well, Sydney was sitting. Tom was pacing the room like a caged panther long overdue for his feeding. She wanted to cry so badly, she could taste her tears in the back of her throat. It was terrifying and humiliating to be handcuffed, photographed, fingerprinted, and interrogated like a common criminal when she'd never so much as been sent to the principal's office before. She hadn't ever had a parking ticket. She wanted to cry, and she would have if it weren't for Tom.

"I'm sorry," he said, moments after they'd been brought together again and locked into the small room with a bare, unwelcoming table and four equally disagreeable chairs. "I should have checked the car out before I signed for it."

"You couldn't have known it was used in a robbery," she said, weak with worry—her second career.

"I should have thought of the probability of it, though," he said tersely. "Why else would they have left it in one piece? They were going to come back for it."

"I can't believe this is happening to us. I thought our luck had changed."

"This is more than bad luck. This is . . ." He shook his head as if their ill-fated fortune defied a definition. He closed his eyes and rested his head on the wall behind him. She didn't have the heart to add her tears to his misery.

It was shortly after that that he began walking the short distance between the door and the wall, without uttering another word and quickly glancing away whenever their gazes happened to meet.

In silence they waited, two tattered and drained desperadoes, until Tom's attorney was shown into the room.

He was a tall, distinguished-looking man in his

late fifties or early sixties and, knowing a few attorneys herself, not at all the sort of person Sydney could connect with Tom. He was a somber person, who listened to them retell their tale of woe without the slightest spark of compassion or understanding in his demeanor. As a matter of fact, she got the distinct impression that he didn't believe a word of what they were saying.

Still, when all was said and done, he left them with the promise that he would see what he could do about expediting their immediate release.

"Nice guy," she said in a sarcastic monotone, with barely enough energy left to turn her head and look at Tom.

"The best," he said with utter confidence, obviously misconstruing her words. "We'll be out of here in no time."

Sydney didn't think so. She was resolved to the idea of going to jail. It seemed a fitting and proper end to the evening they'd spent together. The perfect ending to their perfect date.

Her thoughts swirled like a whirlpool, spiraling downward into a dark abyss. She first thought of how her going to jail would affect her parents, then her career. And as she so frequently saw on television, innocent people *were* sent to prison. It could happen, she pestered herself, at which point her mental images took a sharp dive toward the bottom, toward beatings, white slavery, rape, and, of course, death.

"No time at all," had been Tom's estimation of the period in which it would take his attorney, Mr. Edgewater, to procure their release. Comparatively speaking, the half hour they had to wait was nothing at all . . . except for the silence.

Sydney tried to initiate a conversation with Tom once or twice, but it was becoming more and more evident that whatever it was that was bothering him—and she didn't think it was the misunderstanding with the police—was now getting the best of him.

He would answer in monosyllables, which in itself didn't bother her as much as the way he couldn't seem to bring himself to look at her when he muttered them. As a matter of fact, it was beginning to irritate her.

Hadn't she been through as much as he had that night? Weren't her nerves as raw as his? Hadn't she been frightened, hurt, humiliated, and locked up in jail alongside of him? Hadn't she had her hopes for the evening? And hadn't they been battered and bruised as badly as his? So how come she'd come to know him and to trust him . . . to love him, in fact, and he couldn't share his pain with her?

The longer the silence continued between them, the madder she got at being excluded from whatever he was brooding about. It was a little crazy, she knew, but it had been a crazy night and she was crazy in love with him. She'd never been in love before, not in the way she loved Tom. And if being restricted from his thoughts and feelings when he was so obviously upset about something was his way of showing her that he cared for her as well—well, he had another think coming.

"What *is* the matter with you?" she asked point-blank, the tone of her voice bringing his glance her way. "Have we fallen in love with each other or not?"

At last she had his full attention. He stopped his pacing and looked at her as if he'd forgotten she was in the room and was surprised to see her sitting so nearby.

"Well?" she said, standing to put her hands on her hips. "I'm waiting. Are we in love or not?"

He frowned. A glimmer of his spirit shone in his eyes, and his lips began to twitch into a lopsided grin. "Why do you ask?"

"Because I want to know. Because I've been dreaming about falling in love since I was a little girl, and I have certain expectations and conditions I want met."

His brows rose with amusement and interest. "Like what?"

"Well," she said with some consideration, "I expect it to be a sharing thing. Rich and poor. Good and bad. I don't expect to be happy all the time. I expect problems. I expect the person I fall in love with to share my troubles with me. And I expect to share his."

He wasn't laughing anymore. He was in love. She didn't know what she was asking for, of course, but he liked the way she was thinking. If she hadn't looked so dead serious about her demands, he'd have grabbed her up and kissed her until she went limp in his arms—and even then he wouldn't have let go of her.

As it was, he locked his fingers behind his back to resist the temptation and walked several steps closer to her. "What if this other person's problem could destroy the love between you? Would you still want to hear it?" he asked.

She pondered his questions, wondering what could be so awful that it could destroy love. "Would it be something so horrible, it couldn't be forgiven?" she asked.

"No. It's more like something that would have to be lived with. Always there, out in the open."

She was starting to wish that she hadn't brought it up, when she looked at him and saw the hesitation and regret in his eyes. He plainly wanted to tell her, but . . . What could possibly be so awful?

Due to her nature, she'd never considered herself a particularly brave person. There were risks one took and risks one avoided, for fear of death. But also due to her nature, she'd come to know her limitations fairly well. She knew when she could trust someone and when she couldn't. And she was beginning to recognize what it meant to be in love. She loved Tom, and she had faith in him. There wasn't a doubt in her mind about his goodness or his integrity. There wasn't anything about him that she couldn't learn to live with. She was sure of it.

"I'd want to know," she said firmly, looking him straight in the eye.

The gentlest of smiles came to his lips, and the warmth in his eyes settled deep within her, spreading its heat to remote, untouched places in her heart and soul. She wanted to reach out and touch him, comfort him. But his misgivings wouldn't allow it.

"Let's sit," he said, motioning to the chairs, thinking she wouldn't have so far to fall when she went into convulsions after hearing what he had to tell her.

They sat on opposite sides of the table, their fingers automatically seeking and finding the other's. She watched him intently, braced for whatever words came out of his mouth while he mentally debated the best place to start.

"I was going to tell you earlier," he said, and then he corrected himself. "I wanted to tell you earlier, but I never know how people will react, so I usually wait until I know them a little better before I say anything. In your case, I waited too long." He paused. "But I suppose if I'd told you sooner, we wouldn't be sitting here now anyway, so I guess it's just as well I didn't tell you right away."

Sydney sighed. Sooner, later, now. She had a feeling that whatever he wanted to tell her would have taken forever no matter when he'd chosen to tell her.

"But later, after . . . at the hospital, I knew I'd have to be very careful and pick the right time and the right place and the right words to tell you."

She nodded. It was a nod of encouragement, not understanding. He was taking so long in telling her that her sense of humor was coming back. She recognized a worried person when she saw one, and she laughed inside at the thought of two intense worriers living in the same house, locking the same door twice, checking the unplugged coffee pot over and over again . . .

He looked around the room, released a short laugh, and then continued. "This isn't exactly the place I had in mind, and it's probably not the right time, after all we've been through tonight, but I've got to tell you. You have a right to know before we get any more involved with each other."

"Okay. I'm listening," she pointed out.

"It's about my job, Sydney. What I do for a living."

She gasped dramatically and pulled her hands away, crying, "You *are* the state executioner!" But when he looked shocked and horrified by her remark, she took his hands back into her grasp and shook them. "Tom, lighten up. What could be so terrible? But I trust you, and I know that whatever it is, we can work it out together."

The door opened, and Mr. Edgewater stepped into the room.

"Not now, Peter," Tom said, holding his hand in

the air to ward off the attorney. "We need a few more minutes alone."

The stony-faced man stood in the doorway holding his briefcase. Only his eyes moved as he slowly surveyed their surroundings. He apparently found nothing that caught his interest, and he returned his steady stare at Tom. "You're free to leave whenever you choose, Thomas," he said.

"Thanks," Tom said with only a cursory glance at the lawyer, his attention riveted on Sydney and her reaction to what he had to tell her.

Sydney, however, was rather impressed with the attorney's accomplishment.

"That's it?" she asked. "We're free to go? That's wonderful. Mr. Edgewater, you're wonderful."

He shook his head as he disclaimed the compliment. "No great feat, Ms. Wiesman. I simply retold the story as you told it to me and explained to the officer in charge that Mr. Ghorman had a reputation to protect and that he was hardly the sort of person who would risk his family name and business burglarizing pawnshops."

"A reputation to protect?" she asked, smiling as she looked at Tom. Ministers and politicians had reputations to protect. Teachers, lawyers, doctors, policemen . . . Lord, there were any number of professionals who dealt in human services and needed to keep their reputations clean. What was he so worried about? she wondered.

"It's no big deal," Tom said, dismissing the lawyer and his statement with a few careless words.

"I beg to differ, Thomas," the austere gentleman said, arching one eyebrow in disapproval. Sydney was grateful her father had never learned to use such facial expressions and pitied the man's children—if he'd ever worked up enough enthusiasm to have any.

"Don't," Tom said, but too late to keep the man from speaking his piece.

"Ghorman and Sons is a distinguished and reputable institution in this city, Thomas. And a name is only as good as its reputation. It's important to consider—"

"Ghorman and Sons?" Sydney broke in, her confusion exposing her to the lawyer's harsh stare.

He looked at her as if to say that he was well aware of the fact that he never stuttered over his words and that she had indeed heard him correctly, but he repeated himself nonetheless.

"Ghorman and Sons," he said. "It has an impeccable reputation."

"Ghorman and Sons?" she repeated, this time in disbelief, her gaze moving slowly in Tom's direction.

Tom swallowed hard and frowned with foreboding as he watched her. He could almost see the gears in her mind begin to grind and shoot sparks of recognition. Her silence made his ears ache. His heart felt like lead, sinking low in his chest. He wanted to hide from her, but he wanted to be with her more. He wanted to touch her, but he was afraid of what she'd do.

"You're Ghorman and Sons?" she asked in a deceptively quiet voice.

He nodded once. "Actually, I was an only son, but my father was an ambitious man." He tried to smile, but it was more of a pained grimace. "Now . . . now I'm Ghorman, and I'm ambitious."

In a louder but a fairly even tone of voice, she said, "You're the Ghorman and Sons on my desk, back at my office?"

He was glad she'd brought that up. He'd been

planning to explain the coincidence. "Yes. But it was just a fluke that you'd be the one auditing my business. I didn't know. I can't add more than three numbers in a row, so I leave all that stuff to my accountant. And the reason I didn't explain who I was right away was because it was obvious that you hadn't made the connection with my name, and I figured there'd be time to explain it all—"

"You're the Ghorman and Sons of Ghorman Mortuaries?" she broke in, her voice tight and a little shrill as she stood and looked down at him, appalled.

"Yes. But it's not what you think, Sydney." He stood as well, to be on a level with her. Physically anyway. Spiritually he could feel himself sinking deeper and deeper into a hole from which there was no escape.

Sydney's world was reeling off its axis. She had only one question left to ask, and she didn't want to hear the answer. She wished she'd never heard the name Ghorman before. She wished she didn't already know who he was and what he did. She wished their night together had never happened and that she hadn't gotten out of bed the day before. She wished . . .

"You're a mortician!" she shouted, making it sound like an accusation. "You knew. You knew about me. You knew what you were. And you didn't tell me?"

"You didn't tell her?" Edgewater reiterated from the doorway.

"I was waiting for the right moment," Tom said, addressing himself to the lawyer, who at least appeared willing to listen to reason. Sydney was staring at him as if he'd suddenly taken on the persona of the Grim Reaper.

"You should have told her, Thomas."

"Well, I know that," he said, running an agitated hand through his hair. "I was going to, but I didn't know if she was some sort of kook who'd think I had the inside track on the next world or not. And by the time I'd decided that it was okay to tell her, there was the thanatophobia thing to get around, and then we were arrested. . . ."

"The what to get around?" Edgewater asked.

"Thanatophobia," Sydney answered on her way to the door. "I'm a kook who's afraid of dying."

Tom could see she was leaving and rushed after her. "That's not what I meant, Sydney. I don't think you're a kook. You have a mental disorder. No. An emotional problem. That's not it either," he called after her as she walked out the door. "A hang-up is all it is. We can work it out."

Of all the men in the world, the most exciting, understanding, and compatible man she'd ever encountered turned out to be the nemesis to her greatest fear. And she was stupid enough to have picked him, stupid enough to have fallen in love with him, and certainly stupid enough to have volunteered for the game show in the first place.

But it wasn't television anymore. It was life. Television had magic and a way of making things perfect. Television had actors who pretended to be someone they weren't for ten hours a day and then went home to their real lives, separating life from fantasy. But how could she separate a real man from his real profession? Actors were actors. CPAs were CPAs. Morticians were morticians. It would be like trying to dissect the soul from the body . . . like death.

"Sydney, wait," Tom called. "I didn't mean what I said. It's not that big a problem. We can work it out."

"Go to hell," she said without turning around, needing to lash out at someone for her stupidity, trying to focus on the door at the end of the hall through the tears in her eyes.

The last thing she heard as she walked out the door was Tom's irritated voice. "Go to hell? Go to hell? I thought this was hell!"

Eight

Rex Swann sat staring at Sydney in astonishment and disbelief.

"The police handcuffed you and took you to jail?" he asked.

Sydney nodded.

He turned to look up at Tom, whose expression was attentive but guarded.

"Tom. Tell me the two of you made this up. Tell me it didn't really happen," Rex said, his comic incredulity and amazement causing the audience to howl with laughter.

Tom chuckled in his good-natured way and shrugged helplessly. "Every word of it is true, Rex. It was a date unlike any other—and one I won't soon forget."

The audience roared, and for the first time in her life, Sydney wished she could die. She would have gladly embraced it, in fact, had the crowd and Rex Swann known the whole truth.

Between the two of them, she and Tom had told the major events of their date, omitting such minor details as her reaction to being stuck in the elevator and her subsequent indulgence with Jerry's flask; her vomiting at the sight of Tom's blood; her irrational behavior at the hospital; and the hurtful accusations at the police station. Despite the apprehensions she'd had before the taping began, Tom had very kindly refrained from mentioning her phobic illness—which dismayed and confused her all the more.

Shame and remorse had become her constant companions in the two weeks following their disastrous date. She hadn't gotten back to her apartment that morning before she realized what she'd done. Bewildered and hurt, she had allowed her fear to take control and had denied Tom his one request—an understanding of his profession. To top it off, her imagination had conjured up an image of Tom in a rage, thirsty for revenge. Yet he had allowed his best opportunity to punish her go by without the slightest slur against her. Not only had she hurt him, she had misjudged him, she realized now. She felt lower than low.

"Obviously you weren't sent to prison," she heard Rex Swann speaking to Tom. "Or we'd be having this discussion from behind bars. Although it seems as if that's the way this date should have ended." He paused to let the audience enjoy his humor. "Tell us how the date did end."

"The police were quick to realize that there'd been a misunderstanding, and we were released," Tom said simply.

Sydney felt like worm spit.

"Did you try to continue the date after that?" Rex asked.

"No. Ah . . . we were both pretty tired," Tom said with a small smile. "Calling an end to the evening seemed like the best thing to do."

Rex turned to Sydney with sympathy etched on his face.

"I'm speechless," he said. But he didn't hesitate to continue. "That has to have been the world's worst date. Was there any romance at all?"

She glanced at Tom and back to Rex before answering. "Yes. Some."

"Well, quickly tell us about that," he said eagerly.

"We . . . um . . . we talked quite a bit and got to know each other pretty well."

"Any kissing? Any good stuff?"

"Yes. Some."

"Any sparks there?" He sounded hopeful. "Did this date have any redeeming qualities?"

"Yes. Some."

"Yes, some what? Sparks or redeeming qualities?"

Again she looked up at Tom. "Both," she said.

"Ah-ha! So it wasn't a complete bust. Would you like to see who the audience voted to be your date?" he asked.

She didn't really have a choice in the matter. Stills of the three videos she'd had to choose from were displayed somewhere for the television audience, and a tally was run with the number of votes showing up in each picture on the monitor in the studio.

"Oh, look. The audience chose Tom too." Rex grinned at her. "If you'd like to live dangerously and ask Tom out again, we'll pay for the date. If not, you're on your own."

There would be no sleeping or eating for Sydney until she was alone with Tom one last time. She didn't think she could bear to go out on another date with him, but continuing the way she had for the two weeks she'd spent obsessing about him would be far worse.

He'd consumed her every thought. Food lost its flavor and lay heavily in her midsection, as if she'd swallowed an anvil. Her nights were restless and plagued with dreams of his kisses, his touch, and the twinkle of humor in his eyes. She had to see him one more time. She needed to make peace with him, or he'd haunt her for the rest of her days.

"We, ah, wouldn't have to come back and talk about it, would we?" she asked, before she acted on the impulse that was teasing her brain. Over Rex's shoulder, she saw Tom's confusion. Plainly, he had expected her to scream hysterically at the very suggestion of a second date with him.

"No. Not if you didn't want to. Although I'd personally love to hear how a second date between the two of you turned out," Rex said, encouraging the people in the studio to agree with him. Which they did readily.

"Well, if it's okay with Tom, I would like to see him again," she said bravely, all too aware that he might refuse to have anything to do with her.

This was his chance to humiliate her on national television and get even with her for embarrassing him at the police station. This was his opportunity to snub her and hurt her. This was his opening to show a complete lack of understanding and compassion that was as great as her own.

"I'm game," Tom said, deftly hiding his bewilderment from those who didn't know him as well as Sydney did.

The crowd let out a whoop that very nearly drowned out Rex's amplified approval. "That's the spirit," he said. "Come on out here, Tom."

The screen behind Rex went blank while both he and Sydney stood in anticipation of Tom's appearance on stage. Of course, Rex's anticipation was well rehearsed and a part of every show he did. Sydney's felt more like a riot in the pit of her stomach, threatening a total revolt at any moment.

Tom stepped from behind the false wall onto the stage and shook hands with Rex before approaching her. As she'd been the first time she'd seen him, Sydney was struck by how much more lifelike he was in person than on the video screen—bigger than life, actually.

A camera wasn't capable of capturing the magnitude of the man. It couldn't reveal his appeal. The dignity in his shoulders or the integrity in the way he held his head. It missed the way he bent to hear all that Rex was saying, as if there were a value to each word spoken to him. It couldn't catch the fluid step and easy carriage that made him seem so open and approachable. Or the astute light in his eyes that gave away his intelligence and understanding. A camera couldn't see all the dimensions of the man, couldn't give the man's picture his spirit. But Sydney saw it. And she could feel it. Maybe that was why she couldn't meet his gaze directly.

There was a brief, awkward hug between them, though neither one was inclined to show affection for the other. But it seemed expected—if for no other reason than to show their good sportsmanship.

In an unspoken, mutual agreement they reserved any personal discussion until after Rex Swann had wished them better luck on their next date, asked them to keep in touch, and then prepared the studio and television audiences for a commercial break.

A small swarm of employees gathered about Rex to powder his nose and brief him on the next segment of the program, while the young man in the headset motioned Tom and Sydney off the stage.

"That was great, folks. Really great," he said, handing Sydney a sealed envelope. Looking at her more directly, he added, "No wonder you didn't want to go on. I'd want to forget the whole thing ever happened too."

Neither contestant commented.

Sydney felt as if she were a robot. She walked. She talked. She smiled. There were thoughts in her head, but none of them had anything to do with her actions. She signed the voucher, shook hands with the young man in the headphones, and said good-bye before it occurred to her that she shouldn't be taking the money. She had no intention of going out on another date with Tom.

"I, no, oh, wait," she called to the young man, waving the white envelope. He walked around a corner and didn't see or hear her. "Nuts."

"What?"

In another involuntary movement she looked at Tom and abruptly realized that they were alone.

For a man who had mastered the art of hiding most of his fears and concerns, he was a bust at masking his anger. Where his eyes had once held the warmth and happiness of a summer sky, they now held the cold, chilling bleakness of winter.

"I, ah, I shouldn't have signed for this money. I shouldn't have taken it," she said, faltering, her breath coming in short anxious bursts.

"Why not? You shouldn't pay for a date you don't want," he said. Again, she looked into his features to find the gentle, laughing man she'd come to know and care for, the man she'd hurt—but he wasn't there.

"I am right, aren't I?" he asked, although it

wasn't really a question. "What was that out there? An act to show the world that in spite of the fact that we had the world's worst first date, you still think I'm someone worth dating? Some pretense to spare me embarrassment? Or have you changed your mind about what I do for a living?"

"No. I . . . it's not that. I needed to talk with you."

She'd dialed his home number a hundred times in the previous two weeks, only to hang up before the connection was made. Just as many times she'd hoped to bump into him somewhere. She'd needed to talk to him so badly, so many times. And now that she could, the words she'd prepared and practiced seemed dull and inadequate.

"I did want to see you again," Sydney finally said.

"On a date?" He was stunned.

"No. But I wasn't sure what would happen if I said I didn't want to go out with you a second time. I mean, I didn't know if you'd leave the studio and I'd never see you again, or if we'd have another opportunity to talk. I . . . I've been wanting to apologize to you."

"For what?" His angry tone didn't waver. It was as if she'd committed so many crimes against him, he wasn't sure which she was referring to.

"For the way I behaved at the police station. For not understanding about your profession. I . . . it was the one thing you asked for on your video, understanding, and . . . I wasn't. I'm sorry."

Lips that she knew could be outstandingly kissable, that could transport her to a land of cloud castles and knights on white steeds, were hard and unforgiving as they parted and then came together again determinedly.

"We do need to talk," he said thoughtfully. His voice was quieter but still brittle and tight with his ire. He wasn't about to give her amnesty. Not yet anyway. Nor could he afford to allow himself to feel hope. She wasn't exactly throwing herself into his arms.

The envelope in her hands caught her attention. She held it up to him. "I could buy us both a fifty-dollar cup of coffee," she said, lamely trying to lighten the atmosphere between them.

He eyed the envelope for a second or two and then shook his head as he took it from her.

"Dinner. Tonight. After our first date, we owe ourselves a last date, don't you think?"

"I don't know, Tom," she hesitated. "Do you really think that's such a good idea? Aside from our personal differences, the gods don't seem to like us much." A soft, nervous laugh escaped her. "In fact, I think they're out to get us."

"You don't really believe that, do you?"

She shrugged. She wasn't sure what she believed anymore.

"It seems as logical as everything else I've been thinking lately," she admitted, knowing instinctively that despite his anger and all that had passed between them, she could still trust him with her thoughts and emotions. "I'm really confused."

"Good," he said, more pleased with her bewilderment than with her apology. "Tonight at seven, then. I'll pick you up. Home or office?"

"Home," she said, and then hastily added, "But I could meet you somewhere."

"Too complicated. We tried that the first time, remember?"

"Having you pick me up didn't work out too well either."

"Didn't it?" His eyes narrowed slightly as he studied her, then he quickly glanced at his watch.

"Look," he said, in an immediate hurry. "I have to go. Be ready at seven and—we'll work it out then. Dress casual."

"My address—"

"I've driven past your apartment building a hundred times in the past two weeks. I know your address by heart." He started to walk away. But before he'd gotten very far, he turned and retraced the six or eight steps between them.

"The last time we said good-bye, we forgot this part," he said, as he cupped her face with his hands and settled his mouth on hers.

He gave her a pent-up kiss. One he'd been saving for two weeks. Hard, long, and deep, it was a kiss that had had time to ripen and mature. Its flavor was enhanced with passion and need, tangy with its demands. After her initial surprise, Sydney began to savor the kiss, tasting and relishing with gusto, until she grew weak.

"I felt cheated out of that," he said, his voice raspy, his lips still close to hers. She nodded her agreement.

By the time she could force her eyes to open, he was halfway to the exit. He passed Judy in the hall, and she turned to watch him walk away.

"Well, he left grinning, so he can't hate you all that much," Judy said, approaching Sydney with an appraising eye. "So how come you don't look any happier?"

"He's picking me up at seven o'clock tonight. We're going out again."

"That's great!" She took a second look at Sydney. "That is great, isn't it?"

"Ask me tomorrow . . . if I live through it."

Nine

In what seemed to Sydney like only ten minutes, it was seven o'clock. The first time she'd waited for Tom to arrive, the minutes had crawled by. This time, they were whizzing through space like bullets, coming closer and closer to the fatal moment when he would ring her doorbell.

She'd been dreading that moment all afternoon. The more she thought about it, the more she wished she hadn't agreed to go out with him. She simply should have apologized for embarrassing him at the police station and for hurting his feelings, she told herself as she fine-tuned her makeup.

She smoothed down the tight-fitting bodice of the sundress she'd chosen to wear over her slim figure, hoping that Tom wouldn't be able to keep his hands off of her, and praying that a second date with him wouldn't turn out to be the mistake of her lifetime. She slipped on a short matching jacket and moistened her lips with the tip of her tongue—remembering his kiss, craving another, and already regretting the ones she'd missed out on.

"Whoa, mama, look at you!" she heard Judy say when she emerged from the cloister of her bedroom, where she'd spent every second dressing and redressing and redressing again since they'd arrived home from the studio. Her friend shimmied her shoulders and wagged her brows. "If this is the way you dress for a date you're not looking forward to, remind me never to double-date with you and someone you're crazy about."

"Too much?" Sydney asked. She looked at the dress ambivalently. She was perfectly willing to change into something drab and depressing.

"No. It's perfect. You'll knock him dead."

Sydney looked horrified.

"For crying out loud, it's a figure of speech," Judy said, her tolerance for Sydney's self-imposed misery obviously growing thin. "You've got to stop this. Think of him as a man, not a mortician. There's more to him than just his job. You said so yourself. You spent twelve straight hours with him and never once guessed what he did for a living. You didn't even talk about his job because you had so many other things to talk about."

"Yeah, like how we were going to survive the night," Sydney replied sarcastically.

"That was a fluke. It'll never happen again. Tonight will be calm and peaceful."

"Dull, you mean. And then we'll run out of things to say and start talking about our jobs . . . Oh, why did I agree to do this?" she wailed, flopping down on the couch beside Judy like an old dish rag. "I just should have said I was sorry and run away."

"I really hate to sound like somebody's mother,

but—" July raised her voice and whined the words—"running away is no answer."

"There is no answer."

"Sure there is," her friend insisted. "Go out with Tom and see if it's still like magic. If it is, then think of a way to work things out. If the magic is gone . . . well then, it's gone. You won't have to drive yourself nuts anymore."

Judy was a down-to-earth, straight-thinking person, not unlike Sydney most of the time—which was why they got along so well. At that moment more than ever before, Sydney was grateful for her friendship.

"You're right." In a concise, linear manner Sydney plotted the course of the evening. "I'll go. I'll apologize, and he'll be understanding. He'll be patient and try to explain his job to me. I'll get a clearer picture of what it is exactly that he does as a mortician . . . and then I'll throw up in his lap. He'll get angry—madder than he was this afternoon—and he'll start calling me insane or emotionally disturbed. I'll be offended. I'll call him a . . . a mortician, and he'll be insulted. He'll stalk off and leave me stranded with the tab at the restaurant. I'll call a cab, and it'll be over."

A defeated Judy threw up her hands in exasperation, but didn't have time to speak before the doorbell rang. Sydney groaned.

"Stop that," Judy said, smacking her friend's arm with the back of her hand. "Give it a chance."

Walking to the door, Sydney admitted to herself that she had no other choice but to give the feelings she had for Tom a second chance. While her mind was playing devil's advocate, her heart was firmly set on loving Tom. Where her brain could detect and foresee insurmountable complications arising from the gulf that existed between her nature and his career, her heart vacillated blissfully between not caring and optimistically looking for a bridge that would span the gap between them. And although her thoughts could cause her chest to become heavy and her stomach to ache, her emotions ruled and motivated her.

Expecting to see Tom when she opened the door, Sydney gasped in surprise at the sight of a man dressed in black livery, cap in hand.

"Sydney Wiesman?" he asked in a detached but pleasant voice.

"Yes?"

"Mr. Ghorman has sent a car for you. I'm Wakefield, your driver."

"Oh, this I've got to see," Judy said, jumping up from the couch to the door in one swift motion.

Not knowing what to think or how to feel, Sydney took a firmer hold of her purse and followed the driver.

Judy's giggles and ludicrous facial expressions had little effect on her. She still had reservations about going. Why had he sent a car for her? Wasn't he as eager to see her as she was to see him? Was it a show of power? Had something happened to him? Was it an insult? Or was he trying to impress her, hoping to revive the feelings of affection they'd shared on their first date?

She remained silent until they emerged from the building.

"That's not a . . . a . . ." she stammered, at the sight of a long black limousine parked at the curb.

"A hearse?" Judy supplied the word for her.

"But . . . but . . ." Sydney was too stunned to speak.

Judy, however, had no difficulty understanding her. "Will you relax? The family rides in the limousine. You have to be able to sit up and breathe to ride in the limousine." She motioned for the perplexed driver to open the door. Giving her pal an encouraging headlong nudge into the back of the limo, she slammed the door closed before Sydney could turn around and get out again. Bellowing from the other side of the tinted window, Judy added, "It's you, Sydney! You were born to ride in a limousine."

Sydney seriously doubted it, but there wasn't a whole lot she could do, short of throwing a hysterical fit—which she refused to do. She was determined to see Tom and finalize their relationship one way or another. And if the mountain wouldn't come to her, she'd have to ride to the mountain in a black limousine. That's all there was to it, she decided firmly, actively avoiding the driver's curious glances through the rearview mirror, wishing the interior wasn't as black and solemn looking as the exterior.

Some thirty minutes later, Tom's face passed briefly through Sydney's field of vision, and then she heard him say, "What's the matter with her? What happened?"

"I don't know, sir," a male voice replied. "She looked okay when we left, but she kept muttering things like 'I wish it were white,' 'I can do this,' and 'This isn't what it looks like.'" He shrugged. "I tried talking to her, but she kept on muttering, and after a while she stopped and got all glassy eyed. That's when I called and asked you to meet us here. I wasn't sure of what to do for her."

Tom bent and peered into the limo at Sydney. "Help me pry her out, will you? I think she'll be okay once she's out in the open and gets some fresh air."

With the driver pushing from one side and Tom pulling from the other, they managed to get her to the door.

"Come on, sweetheart. You're okay," Tom said, coaxing her through the opening. "This wasn't such a hot idea, was it?"

Like a zombie, she stood up beside the limousine, staring at the top button of Tom's white shirt, hearing but not thinking or feeling. Mental and emotional shutdown had been her only defense against her overactive imagination and her overreacting senses.

"I'm sorry," he said. "This is my fault. I should have guessed you'd connect a black limousine with—" he paused as he caught sight of the driver, who was standing several feet away and taking in the scene with less concern than curiosity.

"Thanks, Wakefield. She'll be fine, so you can take off now. I'll take her home myself." His dismissal left the driver no alternative but to tip his hat and bid his employer a good evening before he drove away.

"There. It's gone now," Tom said, turning his attention back to Sydney.

They were alone in the parking lot above a private marina in Alamitos Bay. A breathtaking sunset was at its peak. The Supreme Artist had fused fuchsia, gold, and blue in a unique and perfect fashion, a once-in-a-lifetime, never-to-be-seen-again spectacle—but neither of them seemed to notice.

"Sydney, look at me," Tom said, touching her face, soothing her with hand and voice. "I'm sorry. I thought you'd feel safer if I didn't come to pick you up, and a taxi seemed out of the question, so I . . . look at me, Sydney."

Her eyes moved slowly in his direction, taking on a slow light of recognition.

"Bright pillows," she muttered.

"What?"

"Bright pillows." Her tongue grew more limber with the exercise. "It's all black. Bright-colored pillows would help."

Tom laughed, both in relief and at what was apparently her last rational thought before her mind had closed up shop.

"You know, I think you're right," he said, making a mental note to have all the interiors of his limousines redecorated. "Black is depressing, and the last thing in the world we need more of is depression. Whoever said that in keeping with decorum, everything had to be black?"

"Not me. Those silver-gray limousines are nice too," she said, closing her eyes and trying to clear the fuzziness in her head. She felt at a distinct disadvantage having to spend her first few moments with Tom regrouping her senses. But of all the people in the world to be at a disadvantage with, Tom would always be her first choice.

She had great faith in Tom's understanding and patience. From the moment she'd shared her secret with him, he had been nothing but compassionate. Tested by betrayal, anger, and pain, his integrity had never faltered.

"What's this?" she asked when she began to take note of her surroundings. She felt Tom's arm loop around her waist as he turned her toward the sunset and the flotilla of seagoing vessels below.

"This is Plan B. Remember? If you didn't like me, I was going to win you over with my boat?" he said.

His words hit her like a gut punch.

"Tom. I *do* like you. I . . . I like you very much. What happened at the police station wasn't personal."

"It wasn't?"

"No. I mean, it wasn't your fault. It was mine. It was a blind reaction to your being a . . . a . . ."

"Mortician? Undertaker?" He didn't seem the least bit perturbed by her inability to accept his profession. In fact, he was teasing her about it.

"Well, yes," she said, bewildered by his behavior. "I can't tell you how sorry I am that I let myself react without considering . . . How sorry I am that I hurt you."

"Sure you can. But let me show you my boat first." He had her by the hand and was pulling her down the planks that led to the docks.

"You don't have to do this, you know. Having a boat isn't going to change the way I feel about you," she said, trotting along behind him to keep up with his long, hurried strides.

"You mean, I don't stand a chance—ever? No matter what?" he asked, coming to a sudden halt.

She didn't see the expression on his face. She'd collided nose first with his chest and was busy trying to right herself and answer him at the same time. If she had seen his face, she would have seen the glint of determination in his eyes and the stubborn set of his jaw and given up then and there.

"No. That's not what I meant."

"I do have a chance, then," he concluded.

She stood back and saw that his eyes were filled with laughter and what could only be described as supreme confidence. It was baffling. It shook her own confidence to its core. He was a man with a plan. And she was the nucleus around which he'd designed his ambitions.

"There *might* be a chance for us," she said carefully.

A shockingly cocky grin quivered across his lips. He turned and began to walk toward the end of the pier again, slowly but still with a tight grip on her hand.

"It's more than just might or maybe, Sydney," he said without a trace of humor. "I admit I had my doubts. I figured it was over the minute you found out I was a mortician. But that was before this afternoon."

"This afternoon?" She let him lead her farther down the pier, wondering what had happened to furnish him with so much assurance. She'd obviously missed something.

"You were confused."

"I'm *still* confused. How does that change anything?"

"It changes our future from an absolute impossibility to a conceivable possibility," he said, guiding her onto a four-foot walkway between two large sail craft. "Your confusion is an open invitation for me to persuade you to start thinking my way."

"Oh yeah?" she said, responding to the challenge he was presenting her. "And what exactly is your way of thinking?"

His gaze captured hers and held it fast, proving the seriousness of what he was about to say.

"We belong together," he stated firmly, leaving no room for an if, and, or but. "What do you think of her?" he asked abruptly, sweeping a hand out over the boat on their right before she had time to argue.

In a state of denial—spiked heavily with yearning—she watched him step down onto the deck of the boat. He turned to help her, holding his arms out expectantly, seeming to know that she wouldn't run, that she'd leap into his arms anytime he asked her to.

It was true, of course. As much as she wanted to feel in control of the situation, she knew in that instant that she wasn't in control of anything—her mind, her heart, the circumstances. She was a willing victim of the moment, a fatality to a power far greater than any she possessed . . . a casualty of love. She stood on the dock and looked at Tom, acknowledging in her heart that she loved him more than anything else in the world.

There were no bells, no firecrackers. Nothing was as she had expected it to be. After all the years of wanting and wishing for love, all she felt was a bittersweet soreness in her chest that was deeper and truer than anything she'd ever felt before.

Unable to disappoint him, she placed her hands on his shoulders and allowed herself to be lifted, then lowered to the deck beside him.

The double-mast schooner, with its gleaming white planks, varnished oak trim, and polished brass, was obviously well loved and cared for. It was a beautiful vessel. One Sydney normally would have gotten extremely enthusiastic over. But she wasn't looking at the sleek, lean lines of the hull and the height of the masts and imagining herself sailing with the wind in her face.

She was watching the strange look in Tom's eyes. The tenacity she saw played with the muscles of her stomach; the possessiveness made her throat feel tight. But the tenderness and wonder left her heart fearless and her pulse racing.

"Want a tour?" he asked, his gaze taking a leisurely trip along the planes of her face, resting briefly on her mouth, and then detouring south to her breasts.

"Sure." The fluttering in her chest was making her dizzy.

It was all there—the stern, the bow, the halyard, the moon, the end of the sunset, and the stars as they began to glitter and glow in the dark. He told her about the depth sounder and the direction indicator, and she tried to appear interested. What she heard was the lapping of the water, an occasional gull overhead, and the ruckus her heart was making.

"Tom, it's beautiful. It really is," she said, sliding a hand over the smooth oak wheel. "I'm envious."

"She sails better than she looks." He grinned and leaned back against the wheel. "If you're still here in the morning, we can take her out. Go over to one of the islands and spend the day maybe."

"That sounds like another bribe."

"You know it, sweetheart," he said, reaching out to pull her to him. She stood between his legs with her hands braced on his shoulders, his at her hips, and wondered if a man's touch would ever feel as splendid to her.

"I've missed you," he said, relieved beyond belief to have her in his arms once more. "I spent twelve hours with you, and it was as if I'd known you all my life. When you left, I felt . . . lost."

She nodded her understanding, recalling her own sense of disorientation and loss—recalling, too, her reason for leaving.

When he was near her, it was easy to forget what he did for a living. He was too handsome and laughed far too easily to be a mortician, in her book. He was gentle and compassionate, hardly the traits of a man who performed such cold, heartless tasks. Still . . .

"I hear your audit went well," she said, changing the subject, feeling uneasy once again.

He groaned and lowered his head. But when he looked up again, he was laughing at her. "You're going to follow your head and not your heart, huh?"

"Tom, I . . . ." She had to stop. She didn't know what she wanted to say to him. She wasn't even too sure of what she was feeling.

"That's okay," he said, standing, keeping one arm firmly locked around her waist. He wasn't worried. He had his foot in the door, and it was only a matter of time and patience and loving her to distraction before she'd relent and let him into her heart. "I'd rather talk about those conditions and expectations you have about love, but we may as well get this business . . . out of the way. Come see what Rex Swann bought us for dinner. We'll get the talking and eating over with and take our time with dessert."

He smiled at her lecherously and made her laugh. She'd almost forgotten how good he was at that, making her laugh when she least wanted to.

He let her descend first into the well-lit cabin below. The steps were tricky in her pumps, but the trek was well worth it. As clean, elegant, and functional as the vessel was topside, the cabin of the . . .

"I forgot to look at the name," she said, mildly disgruntled. "You can tell a lot about a man by what he names his boat, you know."

He thought her remark over for a second and then agreed. "In this case you're right. Her name's *The Here'n Now*—which is a pretty good title for my philosophy on life too."

"*The Here'n Now,*" she repeated, saying the name as one word the way Tom had. "You don't believe in God and heaven and hell and all that?"

"Sure I do," he said, bending over the small

refrigerator to remove a bowl of tossed green salad and a bottle of white wine. "But it's the here and now that really counts. If getting into heaven hinges on living the best life you possibly can, then this is when you live it—right here, right now. You can't keep worrying about all the mistakes you've made in the past; they're done, you've made them. But you can feel regret and vow to do better—right here, right now. And there's no sense fussing about the mistakes you'll make tomorrow, because—" he hesitated, watching her closely as he finished his sentence, "because there's no guarantee on tomorrow. All you've got for sure is the here and now." He opened the wine with a loud pop. "I figure if you do your best with every here and now you get, you end up with a pretty decent life behind you in the end—and smooth sailing after that, so to speak."

He grinned at her as he handed her a glass of wine and continued with his dinner preparations. She wandered the small confines of the cabin. She didn't get far. The sleeping quarters, along with the compact bathroom, small galley, and eating area, didn't leave much room for nervous wandering.

"I suppose that in your business you'd have to give that sort of thing a lot of thought," she said, pondering a small corkboard where a variety of pictures of friends and family were displayed. "God and heaven and how you live your life, I mean."

"Doesn't everyone? Haven't you?"

She glanced in his direction; he was watching her.

"I avoid thinking about it," she said, slipping into one of the boothlike seats at the table. "When I think of the future, I don't see myself any older than I am at the moment. I don't think of . . . of growing old or of . . . dying. My future is infinite. I don't see an end to it."

Tom nodded, thinking that she was in for a big surprise someday, but liking her way of thinking nonetheless.

"But you don't live in the future, and you're not plagued by your past," he said, knowing her well enough to speculate. "So you live in the present too."

"Pretty much. But I plan very carefully for the future because I know it's coming. If I thought this was the last moment I had on earth, I'd be too afraid to take my next breath."

"And how do you see this never-ending future of yours?"

She shrugged. She couldn't tell him that he was in her picture of the future. She couldn't tell him about the children on the beach or the contentment and happiness she saw for them all. That was her dream of the future, how she hoped it would be. But her experience told her that the future didn't always transpire as she'd envisioned it.

She shrugged again as she answered, "The way it is now, I guess."

"What?" He dropped the salad tongs into the bowl of vegetables and gave her his complete attention. He braced himself on the counter with an arm and a hip and stared at her in suspicion. "Are you telling me that you don't see changes in your life? Ever?"

"No. But—"

"Good. I'm glad to hear it," he broke in. He took on an expression that she was well acquainted with, a tightness in his features that signaled his efforts to control his emotions. Her heart began to skip beats erratically as she recognized the tension and excitement he was battling to contain as he spoke to her. "Because I've got news for you, Sydney. Your life is going to change in a big way, real soon."

Both wary and amused at his presumptuousness, she smiled. She couldn't pretend that she didn't know what he was talking about. Nor could she hide the way it made her feel. She wanted a change in her life, and she wanted it to be him.

"You keep looking at me that way, and this talk is over," he said, pushing away from the counter and taking the seat opposite her. He took her hand in his and caressed each finger in a slow and surprisingly intimate fashion. "I know you're worried and I know you have reservations about us, but I don't. I haven't since the moment I laid eyes on you. So, if you need to talk, talk. I'll answer any questions you have, tell you anything you want to know. But do it now, Sydney, because I want you. And once I make you mine, I won't ever let you go."

She heard herself swallow. Those were the words her heart wanted to hear. He was the man she'd spent her life looking for. She didn't want to talk. She didn't want to worry and fret over something as wonderful as loving and being loved. She didn't want anything but to wallow in the knowledge of his emotions, to relish the warmth in her chest and the excitement deep in her belly. But how often did one get what one truly wanted in life?

"Aw, Tom," she lamented. "Can't you see this isn't going to work? It might for a while, sure. While it's new and we can't keep our hands off each other and we're breathing hard and it's easy to forget that there's a whole world out there waiting for us to rejoin it." She paused to take a second breath. "But what happens then? What happens when the new wears off and we want to face the world together? Are you going to want to take me—screaming and wailing—to the Mortician's Annual Fourth of July Picnic? To undertaker conventions? Am I supposed to pretend that I don't know what you do, so that every time I wonder where you are or who you're with, I won't black out or tear out a chunk of my hair?"

"Sydney."

"No. Let me finish." She stood, feeling the need to move. She felt as if she were about to burst from the nervous tension and dejection inside her. "Do you know that I blacked out at that hospital you took me to? I don't remember anything past those two metal doors. Not the jokes or the doctor or the X rays . . . not even you. If we stay together, I'd be blinking in and out of reality every time I asked you something as simple as how your day went."

"Not if you knew what my day was really like," he said, turning to watch her pace the small confines of the cabin. "I'm just an ordinary businessman. I have an office, secretary, everything. The funeral homes run themselves. I have very little to do with them anymore."

"But you're a mortician."

"What's that?" he asked. "You've got it in your head that being a mortician hasn't changed in the past two hundred years. But it's just like every other profession. It's all specialized now. There are technicians, hairdressers, makeup artists, funeral directors, PR people, accountants. You name it, we got it. It's a family business that I inherited from my father. I go to the office every day and push papers around on my desk. That's it."

"Where is your office?" she asked, as if it might be a factor worthy of consideration.

He grimaced. "Right now, it's downtown at the original parlor. But I could always move to a regular office building," he added quickly. "Would that help?"

"I don't want to turn your whole world upside down," she said, throwing her hands up in despair. "It wouldn't be fair. I'd feel worse than I do now."

She picked up a pretty pink conch about the size of her fist and turned it over and over in her hands without seeing it. It was hard to appreciate beauty when one's life seemed dismally futile, when one's happiness was in sight but beyond one's reach.

She heard Tom's movements and didn't reject his touch when he slipped his arms around her from behind. In fact, she sighed and allowed herself to relax and take comfort in the strength and solidity of his body. He pressed his lips to the nape of her neck, and she permitted herself the luxury of wishing he'd do it again.

"It's too late to worry about turning my life upside down, Sydney," he murmured near her ear. "You've managed to spin it around so many times, I can't tell which end is up, anyway."

He turned her in his arms, but when she wouldn't look at him, he placed two loving fingers beneath her chin and forced her gaze to meet his.

"All I know for sure anymore is that I love you, Sydney. For two weeks I tried to talk myself out of the way I was feeling. I told myself it was hopeless, that you'd never accept me because of my profession. I told myself you weren't worth getting all bent out of shape over. I told myself it was an infatuation, that it wasn't anything an hour or two in bed with you couldn't cure. I told myself that it was for the best, that we were never meant to be together. But I don't lie very well. I didn't believe any of it."

A soft laugh escaped him, and he smiled. He

touched her cheek with fingers that were cherishing and filled with the awe he felt inside.

"The battle was over before it was fought," he said. "I pictured my life without you and saw nothing. I couldn't even remember what it was like the day before I met you." She stood mesmerized, hardly breathing, as he spoke and played with the soft blond curls at her temple. "I felt . . . immobilized. I couldn't go back. I couldn't move forward. And every moment without you was empty."

"I know," she uttered, her throat tight around her vocal cords. She knew the empty feeling. She knew the hopelessness that fought with the certainty in her heart. She knew the need of her soul to be with its mate. She knew the ache of her body to be touched, to be one with the man who communicated faith, passion, and belonging to her innermost being.

His kiss was like a field of spring flowers—light, airy, and full of promise. It filled her senses with the warmth of sunshine and the sweet misery of anticipation. Her spirit frolicked in his embrace, and her body grew sensuous and languid against the earthy planes of his body.

"We shouldn't be doing this," she murmured, eyes closed, thoughts spinning. "It'll only complicate things between us."

"Things between us are already complicated." He brushed his lower lip against hers seductively. "This'll help you decide whether or not it's worth fighting for."

It was a lame excuse to have sex with someone, but Sydney didn't need a great deal of justification to do what felt natural and genuine to her.

She was sure that she wasn't the one who groaned like some hungry animal when his lips released hers to wander lazily over her jaw and down her neck—although she was feeling decidedly wild and unbridled inside. He held her, his hands reaching to touch and feel. He pressed her body to his until close wasn't close enough. Each kiss grew deeper, and every gesture was born of an instinct, honed to pleasure her. Even the scent of him seemed to release a new primal urge that she'd never known before.

Her heart chased the sensations that raced through her body. Faster and faster until she was breathless and reeling. Somewhere, in the back of her mind, she knew what was coming. She welcomed it, enticed it.

He slipped the small jacket from her shoulders as she lolled her head to one side to expose more of her neck and shoulder to the overpowering onslaught of his lips to her senses. Her fingers canvassed his thick dark hair, his cheek, and then brought his lips back to hers.

"Do you really think this is a good idea?" she asked with her last bit of recall.

"I think this is the best idea we've had yet," he answered, nuzzling her neck. "I love this dress."

She felt his hand on her bare back and melted in slow degrees.

"There . . . there isn't much to it, is there?" she said, wondering if it had been a wise idea to wear the dress after all. This was the reaction she'd wanted, but . . . "You'd said to dress casual, and I didn't know if you meant casual-casual or casual restaurant—casual."

She sucked in air. Her eyes closed and the strength of her muscles was suddenly on a par with that of a cooked noodle, when he trailed his tongue across her breasts above the bodice of her sundress.

"I meant casual as in anything you don't have to wear pantyhose with. They make me nuts," he muttered, working his way back up her neck to her mouth once more. He fumbled with the zipper of the dress that pressed against her spinal cord. "This little dress is fine for what I had—and still have—in mind."

"What if I'd worn pantyhose with it?" she asked, nervous, needing to distract herself.

"They're not allowed on my boat. You'd have had to take them off before you came on board."

Like her friend Judy, Tom was one of those people who could follow two conversations at once without distraction. Oh, how she envied them. The discourse he was having with her body was distracting in the extreme to the little chat he was having with her verbally. And yet he seemed to be right on top of both of them, with a response for everything.

"What . . . what if I'd refused to take them off?" she asked, as she listened to the whiz of the zipper and felt her dress loosen around her body. She could hear her heart pounding in her ears. She shivered.

"Then getting you naked would have taken me a little longer. Nothing you wore could have stopped this," he said, his voice a husky whisper. He stood back and looked at her. His eyes were bright, like blue fire—consuming, burning, searing away the remains of her doubt.

A gentle, discerning smile curved his lips as he pulled slowly on the straps of her sundress. He was aware of her fears and anxieties. He knew she was as nervous as he was. He took his time to relish the long-awaited moment—to have her naked in his arms—but also to give her one last chance to back away if she felt she had to.

Not that he'd allow her to stay away too much longer, however. And it wasn't as though he was the sort of man who thought sex was the answer to all the world's problems. But if she had more questions to ask or more feelings to get off her chest, he could be put off a while for her peace of mind. Because in his heart, from the depths of his soul, he was so certain of their future together that loving and making love seemed inevitable to him.

His body, of course, was telling him that with his heart set, now was as good a time as any to add the love*making* ingredient to this mystical thing called love. It had suffered the tingles, pangs, and excitement long enough. It was demanding gratification. It didn't care that Sydney was frightened; it was fearless enough for the both of them. It had no tolerance for her qualms and doubts; it wanted her—badly.

And so, with the heart of a man in love and the hands of a man needing to make love, he continued to slowly lower the straps of her dress from her shoulders, waiting for her to stop him, viewing inch after inch of pale golden skin that was too tempting not to touch.

Cool air brushed across her breasts, sensitizing the engorged tissue. The mere thought of Tom's hands on her breasts was enough to harden her nipples.

Deliberately, with the forethought and intent of a seductress, she took a step forward and began to unbutton his shirt.

Sydney had her problems, but she wasn't stupid. She knew when she was beaten. They were going to make love, and there was nothing she could do—nothing she *wanted* to do—to stop it. She was damned if she permitted it to happen, and damned if she didn't. And if she was going to be damned for anything, if she was going to feel sorrow and remorse, it was going to be for an act she had performed—not for what she'd only dreamed of doing. She knew she was asking for trouble. Their loving was impossible. But it was also ordained by fate.

The stress and strain of remaining motionless as he stood and watched her open the front of his shirt and flatten the palm of her hands to the dark spongy hair on his chest radiated from him like waves of heat. She could feel his heart hammering rapidly beneath the smooth corded sinew. It felt powerful.

She shoved his shirt back on his broad shoulders and willfully caught his impassioned gaze. She held it as long as she could as she stepped around behind him to remove the garment from his body. Her hands looked small against the muscled contours of his back. She felt small—small, vulnerable, and eager.

She took the instant needed to lower the sundress the remaining distance to the floor and came to face him in nothing but her best white silk-and-lace panties. Once again she placed both palms to his chest to feel the warmth of his body and the strong, steady beating of his heart.

Their love was a mistake, and yet it was the truest, purest emotion she'd ever known. They had no future, and yet their destiny was to be one through infinity. She shook her head in hopelessness, a prisoner of her own emotions.

"What am I going to do with you?" she uttered in a bare whisper, hardly aware that she'd spoken aloud.

His hands were like fire on ice when they took her upper arms and pulled her closer to him. His face was ablaze with his desire and yearning, but a mere reflection of her own need and longing.

"First, you're going to make love with me," he said. "And then you're going to promise to share your life with me."

It soon became apparent that somewhere in the universe his words were written in stone. Their passion was slow and giving. In a ritual born with the creation of man, they stoked the sacrificial fires and offered their bodies and souls in homage to their love.

His kisses were deep and drugging, stealing away her thoughts. Each stroke of his hand was titillating and tranquilizing to her inhibitions, banishing their power over her. She gave herself freely, offering all she was or would ever be. His mouth closed over the tip of her breast to suckle, and his hand traversed her abdomen, moving slowly downward.

She was weak and aggressive in turn, wavering between insatiable hunger and euphoria. She clutched him to her and then pushed him away, writhing and gasping, desperate for an end to the exquisite agony.

But over and over he drove her to the edge of madness, cruel in his delay, meticulous in his methods. And when she could take no more, when she was about to explode, he saved her. He took her, driving hard and deep, breaking beyond the formidable flames of sensation and the intractable need that was devouring her. She cried out, and he was there, whispering tender, soothing words she didn't recognize and holding her close.

She might not have noticed the gentle rocking of the boat if her body was less attuned to her environment. She emerged slowly from a languorous bliss, feeling alive and highly responsive to the world around her. It was as if she could feel every molecule of air as it rubbed softly against her bare skin.

"Sydney?"

"Mm?"

"What are you thinking?"

She couldn't recall that she *was* thinking. "Nothing, I'm a complete blank."

They were sprawled across the bed in the bow of the boat, legs and fingers entwined. Bracing himself on one elbow, he loomed over her.

"Good. I can begin your reprogramming."

She smiled and opened her eyes to look at him. The strange excitement churned in her abdomen once again. Her body quickened. Lazy fingers touched his cheek to make sure he was real.

"In what way would you like to reprogram me?" She would have done anything he asked at that moment.

"Only one way. A minor detail, really." He kissed her—softly and with deep affection. "Before you have time to start thinking again, I want to fill your head with positive thoughts. I want to firmly fix in your mind how right we are together. There won't be room for any more doubt . . . no more fear."

"Good luck," she said as she began to automatically compute the ramifications of their actions. "I hope you succeed. I want you to."

"But you don't think it's likely." It wasn't a question.

No, she didn't think it was likely. They had a great deal in common, and in their differences he zigged where she zagged in an extremely harmonious manner. But the barrier between them was too large to overcome, too tangible to be tolerated, and too basic to their natures to be ignored. They couldn't change who and what they were, and it was who and what they were that would eventually destroy any happiness they found together.

She sighed heavily as she reached out and pulled him to her. She didn't want to give him up. She knew she would. She knew she had to for both their sakes, but she wasn't ready yet. With his arms around her, their being together *was* right. There were no doubts, no fear. He could make her forget.

"No, I don't think it's likely," she whispered, full of sorrow. "But we have here and now. Isn't it enough that right this minute everything is perfect?"

He pulled back to look at her intently. Here and now was his philosophy more than hers. He knew that even though she lived in the present, she had a careful eye to the future, that she planned for it and counted on its coming. His gaze broke into her soul, and instead of robbing her of anything, he left a deposit. His love. It was like earnest money—collateral on his faith in her good judgment and his trust in her for his own future.

"It's enough for now," he said, bending to press a kiss to her forehead. "We'll live one perfect moment at a time, until we've filled a lifetime with them."

"I hope so," she said, opening her mouth to his next kiss, opening her mind to his persuasion and her heart to his convictions. More than anything else, she wanted to believe in their future the way he did.

Together, with slow, fastidious intent, they assembled minute after minute of perfection. Misgivings gave way to laughter, ecstasy, and intimate whispers in the dark. They lived the future second by second, forming a past, linking their hearts in time.

Ten

"When I can see you again?" Tom asked Sydney early the next morning as they stood outside her apartment door. He had her pinned between the wall and his chest and was determined to have an answer.

"Soon," she said, in no condition to complain about his closeness. There was a sublime ache in rarely used muscles of her body. She was exhausted from a sleepless night. Her mind was weary from thinking too much. And still his kisses excited her, energized her, and removed all thoughts from her consciousness.

All that night she'd known what she had to do. Yet she'd stayed with Tom and selfishly indulged her heart and body. But while she'd lain awake, listening to the soft sounds of water lapping between the dock and the boat and the softer sounds of Tom's respirations in sleep, her thoughts would catch up with her. She would begin to feel guilt and shame. She should have ended the relationship as she had intended to. She should have been stronger. She shouldn't have given in to her desire to make love with Tom. She shouldn't have given him any hope that there was a future for them. Her recriminations had come fast and furious.

And then, on the verge of tears, she'd turned to Tom for comfort, kissing him awake and taking refuge in his strength and love.

"How soon?" he asked, reluctant to leave her, disinclined to give her time alone to think. She made mountains out of molehills better than anyone else he knew, and now that he'd shaved the mountain between them down to its appropriate size, he didn't want to give her time to reinflate it. "Lunch maybe?" he suggested persistently. "Or we could still make it over to Catalina for the afternoon."

"Tom—"

There was a "no" in the tone of her voice, so he cut her off. "Okay, I'll surprise you. Get some sleep, and I'll come back for you at two."

"But—"

This time he stopped her with a kiss. A kiss that left her blurry eyed and stupefied as she stood and watched him walk away. At the elevator he looked back at her and grinned, pleased with his handiwork.

"It's still like magic, I take it," Judy commented moments later, a sly smile on her lips as she watched Sydney fall languorously into the cushions of the couch.

Sydney groaned. "It's worse than magic. I'm in love."

"Too bad," Judy said, being facetious. "Now what are you going to do?"

"I don't know." She yawned loudly. "He's an impossible man. He refuses to listen to reason."

"And you're exhausted from trying to hammer this *reasoning* into his head all night." Again, it wasn't a serious statement.

"Not exactly," she said, peeking out through one eye.

"We're not sending the gentleman mixed messages, are we, dear?" Judy asked, back in her role of somebody's mother.

"They're the only kind I have to send." She swallowed the scream of frustration at the back of her throat. Her voice wavered with emotion when she muttered, "I'm so confused."

"You're not so confused," Judy said, draping an afghan across her friend's body, tucking it under her chin. "Not if you know you love him."

"It isn't as easy as just loving him."

"Loving someone isn't supposed to be easy. Only the falling part is easy. After that it gets a little tougher to make it work and last forever. Now get some sleep. I have a feeling you're going to need plenty of energy to keep up with this impossible man of yours."

Sydney released a long, drowsy sigh. "Mm. I have that same feeling."

She opened her eyes in the twilight and then let them fall heavily back into place. In a half sleep, she was aware of the absolute silence, the comfort, and the warmth and didn't want to disturb any of them. Thoughts knocked softly on the door of her consciousness, but she chose the peace of nothingness as her companion. She drifted in a void, oblivious to the world, her mind's eye a total blank until it suddenly began to flash the message, "Two o'clock. Two o'clock. Two o'clock."

"Oh, no," she cried, throwing off the afghan,

bolting to her feet and scrambling over the back of the couch in one movement. "I'm late."

"Sydney!"

She screamed and turned at the sound of her name. Dusk had shrouded most of the room in darkness. Solid objects were like shadows in the evening's light. Her heart raced while something wild and frenzied surged through her veins.

"Sydney. It's me, Tom."

His solid form moved away from the others to distinguish itself in the half-light, and she went limp with relief.

"You scared the life out of me," she said accusingly, short of breath, patting her chest to calm her heart. "Jeeze, I just hate it when people do that to me."

She walked to the couch and braced her arms against the back of it.

"Sorry," he said, though he didn't sound overly penitent. "Do you always shoot straight up out of a sound sleep like that?"

"No. I was . . . what are you doing here? Where's Judy?" she asked, fully awake at last. She walked around the end of the couch, turned on a low, glowing lamp, and sat down, still feeling a little weak-kneed.

"We had a date, remember?" He sat down beside her.

"Of course, I remember. I . . . what were you doing all this time? Just sitting there?"

"Watching you sleep," he said with a nod of his head. He grinned at her. "Last night I lay awake listening to see if you were going to snore, but I kept falling asleep first."

She'd never known anyone to sit quietly and watch her sleep before. It was disconcerting to say the least. She passed her hand across her mouth and cheek, feeling for dried drool or a woven imprint of the couch covering. She grimaced at the sight of the rumpled sundress she'd been wearing for nearly twenty-four hours and automatically ran her fingers through her hair.

"Judy let you in?" she asked, wondering what she'd done to Judy to deserve this sort of treatment.

He nodded as he watched the play of her emotions in her face. He'd seen everything from happiness to hysteria to pain and pity, but his personal favorite was flustered. Lord, she was cute when she was flustered, he thought, amused.

"And then she left?" She found it hard to believe of a loyal friend.

"I gave her ten bucks and sent her off to the movies."

"And she went?"

"Are you mad?" he asked, hoping he hadn't caused a rift between the two women. Judy had been a fountain of information about her roommate, and he felt indebted to her.

"No. I just . . . Have I ruined our date?"

"No."

"We'll still have time? After I shower?" she asked, eager to make herself presentable, but not necessarily for the general public. Wanting to be with Tom, but not in a crowd.

"Sure."

"Casual?" she asked, eyeing the sweater and jeans he was wearing and the way they defined the hardy musculature of the body she'd come to know so well. Her insides twisted with desire. She wanted to touch him and to feel his hands on her body again.

"Very casual." Hardly worth dressing for at all, he

added mentally, recognizing the smoky look in her eyes.

"Ah . . . well, all right, then," she said, getting to her feet. "I'll only be a few minutes. Can I . . . get you anything?"

"Not right now, thanks," he answered, wanting her to feel comfortable and relaxed before he attacked her and drove her to distraction with his love. Need stirred in his loins as he recalled her metamorphosis from a refined, self-contained young accountant to an untamed, unfettered, and totally unselfish woman the night before.

She turned to leave, then stopped. "Do I? Snore?"

He looked at her and smiled a gentle smile. "No," he said with a shake of his head. "But do you have any idea of what you look like when you're sleeping?"

She was afraid to ask.

"No. What?"

"You look like an angel. Sort of pure and innocent. Untouched and untouchable," he said, a tenderness in his eyes. He hesitated briefly and then added, "I kept thinking that if I'd wanted to, I could have made enough noise to wake you up. But I just sat there . . . watching over you . . . guarding you."

Sydney was too moved to speak. She hadn't really thought about it until that moment, but no man had ever expressed a desire to protect her from anything before—except for her father, of course. Maybe being a smart and self-sufficient career woman led men to believe that she was invulnerable. And to be truthful, she wasn't defenseless. She'd taken care of herself for quite some time and was very capable of continuing to do so. But she felt a warm, secure feeling in her chest, knowing that Tom wanted to protect her.

She smiled at him, and a moment of silent communication passed between them. He seemed to understand that although she didn't need or want him to shelter her from the world, she was glad he wanted to. And he expressed to her that he was someone she could count on if she ever changed her mind.

Lord, the man was getting easier to love all the time. Impulsively she reached out and pressed her palm to his cheek. Where did men as dear and sweet as Tom Ghorman come from? she wondered as she engraved the fine angles and lines of his handsome face and the precise blue of his eyes in her heart.

He covered her hand with his and kissed it. Raw sexual need gripped her low in her abdomen, and her heart fluttered with yearning.

"We could skip the date and go straight to bed," he said, leaving no question as to his frame of mind.

She nodded, but said, "It won't take me long to get ready to go."

Great sex was nothing to base a relationship on, she reminded herself as she finished her toilette with a light coat of lipstick. It wasn't something to spit at, but it wasn't everything. Of course, sex with Tom wouldn't be great if Tom weren't Tom. *He* was everything. She smiled wistfully.

Then her smile drooped. He was everything, including a mortician.

Everyone had faults and flaws. Why couldn't Tom's flaw have been golf? Or laziness? Or a tendency to leave caps off bottles and toothpaste tubes? Why couldn't he have been a plumber or a hair stylist, or worse yet, another accountant?

Why a mortician, of all things? she wondered, opening the bedroom door.

There was a low, glowing light in the middle of the floor, the rest of the room looked dark and empty. She heard music and could smell . . . bread?

"Tom?"

"Turn out the light and come over here," she heard him say from somewhere near the glowing light. She obeyed automatically, her curiosity piqued. "Careful. Watch those bushes there."

"What bushes?" She tripped over a footstool and fell against a chair that wasn't where she had left it.

"Those bushes. Are you all right?"

She laughed. "Where am I?"

"On a grassy bluff overlooking the beach a few miles from my house. It's very romantic here, and you're in the mood to be seduced."

When her eyes adjusted to the light, she could see him on the floor, lying on his side next to what appeared to be one of her lamp shades with a flashlight burning inside of it. Stretching her imagination, she could envision it as a small campfire.

"Do you seduce all your women here?" she asked, sitting Indian style on the floor across from him.

"No. I come here a lot, to think usually. But I've never brought a woman with me before."

"Is that a picnic basket?" she asked.

"Yep. Are you hungry?" He sat up and lifted the lid of the basket. "I brought fresh bread and cheese and fruit and my favorite wine. What would you like?"

"Some bread and cheese and fruit and wine, please."

"Coming right up."

What ensued wasn't like any picnic Sydney had

ever been on before. It was more of a covenant ceremony as they relaxed beside the fire, talking and feeding each other small pieces of food. Head to head, they stretched out on the floor in opposite directions and discussed everything that fluttered through their minds. They wooed each other with the soft tones of their voices, enticed with their eyes, and tempted with gentle touches.

When they made love, it was slow and rapturous. Every caress had a meaning. Every look was significant. They culminated their lovemaking with a silent solemn vow of devotion.

"Sydney?" Tom spoke softly into the near darkness.

"Mm?" she answered, nearly asleep in the warmth and comfort of his arms, wrapped close to him in the afghan he'd taken from the couch.

"I love you."

Her hesitation was marginal, a split-second search of her soul.

"I love you too," she said without a doubt.

There were no further words necessary. And for the next week, no challenge arose to test them. They were inseparable except for their work hours, during which they made frequent calls simply to hear the other's voice.

"We had swings and chinning bars when I was a kid," Tom said, his voice ringing and echoing as if they were in a cathedral. They were facing each other with their legs braced against the opposite wall of a large concrete tube centrally located in the park a few blocks from Sydney's apartment building. "We never had anything like this."

"I wonder why we didn't," she mused aloud.

"This isn't high-tech or complicated. It's a sewer pipe, isn't it? How come we didn't have these?"

"TV was fairly new back then, and they didn't know all the harm it could do, I guess. Now parents have to use their imaginations to figure out ways to keep kids occupied."

"Aren't these the same imaginations that were destroyed in a whole generation of children who sat in front of the television watching *The Mickey Mouse Club* and *American Bandstand*?"

"Yep. The very same."

She crawled out of the tube, saying, "Extremists make me really nervous. Moderation is what I'm going to teach my children. TV is okay if they can read and ride their bike and roller skate and swim too."

"Moderation is good," he agreed, getting to his feet. "But how about supervised moderation?"

"Well, sure. Kids don't know what's good or bad for them until they're taught." Curious, she asked, "Do you want a large or small family?"

"Large."

"How large?"

"Six or eight?"

"Children?" she asked, agog.

"Too many?" he asked, a bit concerned.

Sydney sat in a swing and replayed the vision of her dream family in the back of her mind. She and Tom stood on the deck of the beach house watching the two children playing in the surf. Suddenly a third child in white swimming trunks joined the other two in the sand, and a fourth child, dressed in a white pinafore, came to stand in the billowing folds of her white sundress. Her arm slipped around the little girl's shoulders. She held her close and sighed.

"That's more than I'd planned on," she said to

Tom, still basking in the tranquility of her dream. "But I think I can see my way to managing a couple more."

"Soon?" He pulled the swing back and pushed her high into the air. He smiled when it occurred to him that she'd accepted being the mother of his children without qualm or question.

"How soon?" she asked, looking back over her shoulder at him.

"I could start tonight." He gave her another push and a suggestive grin. "Right now as a matter of fact."

She laughed. "You're that anxious to be a daddy?"

"I'm ready. Now all I have to . . ." His words trailed off as a police car rounded the corner and came to a slow stop in the middle of the street. The men inside eyed the overgrown children in the park suspiciously and pulled the car over to the curb.

"You folks got business here?" one of the officers asked. "There's a curfew posted on this park, you know."

"Ah, no, we didn't know," Tom called back, helping Sydney to stop her swing. "We were just out walking around."

"We'll leave," Sydney added, her last encounter with the police department still fresh in her mind.

"They didn't have curfews on parks either, when we were kids," Tom muttered as they walked away.

"Things are different now," she said, contemplating all the evils that befell children now, that she had never dreamed existed when she was a child. "I want our children to know they're loved and to feel secure."

"They will," he said, pulling her close to his side.

"They'll feel it in us and grow strong in knowing that they're part of us."

She looked at him, and under the streetlights she could see the promise in his eyes. Tom made everything seem right and certain. He had a way of changing the appearance of things. Events that had once looked huge and ominous became simple and as uncomplicated as a walk in the park. He did the most ordinary things in the most romantic of fashions, and what was truly romantic took on a sanctity that was almost spiritual.

"Oh, barf," Judy said a few nights later, groaning in mock disgust. "Watching the two of you make goo-goo eyes over linguini is enough to make a body want to throw up."

Sydney tried to look insulted.

"Goo-goo eyes indeed," she said, glancing at Tom. "Were we making goo-goo eyes at each other?"

"Well, actually, *you* were making goo-goo eyes at me. I was just sitting here, eating my linguini and trying to ignore you."

She sputtered indignantly, giggled, and then sputtered again. He winked at Judy.

"I love it when she's flustered," he said, the loving look in his eyes as he gazed at Sydney bearing a strong resemblance to the aforementioned goo-goo eyes.

"I suppose *men* don't make goo-goo eyes?" Judy said. "And of course, they never get flustered."

"Not real men," he told her, his eyes twinkling as he watched Sydney pick up several dishes from the table and remove them to the kitchen.

"I told you he was impossible," she said over her shoulder to Judy.

Her friend made a remark at which Tom laughed, but Sydney didn't hear it. She was too busy taking note of the warm feelings in her chest. Happy feelings. Contentment. And she was glad she could share some of them with Judy.

So often, female friends were split apart when one or the other fell in love. When one's attention was suddenly diverted elsewhere, the other often felt abandoned and left out—no matter how glad they were that their friend had found happiness. Not so with Judy.

Judy and Tom had formed a different sort of relationship, almost from their first meeting. They saw in each other the qualities Sydney liked best in them and had become friends. They kept a steady stream of teasing banter flowing whenever they happened to meet and seemed to accept the other's presence in Sydney's affections.

Sydney was well aware that now, at last, she had it all. A loving family, good friends, and Tom. And she didn't need a holiday to remind her that she had a lot to be grateful for, she thought, listening to the voices in the next room.

"You know, it's hard to believe you're a . . . ah . . . you know," she heard Judy saying.

"A what?" Tom asked. "A man or a mortician?"

Sydney could almost feel the glances that were being sent her way and quickly busied her hands, pretending not to have heard.

"A mortician," Judy said in a low voice, knowing her friend hadn't as yet resolved her feelings about Tom's job.

They'd carefully avoided mentioning Tom's profession in conversations during the past week. This was the first reference they'd made to it since the night on his boat. Strange, she thought absently, she'd almost forgotten what he was.

"What's so hard to believe?" he asked, not bothering to lower his voice or hide the topic of their discussion. "Morticians are no different from anyone else. We get up in the morning, go to work—we sometimes work odd hours, but then so do cops and doctors and factory workers. We go home to our families, pay taxes, watch football on television. We even have our own jokes."

"Mortician jokes?" she asked.

"Yeah. Want to hear one?"

"Of course."

"A mortician in San Francisco was driving up this hill with a coffin in the back of his hearse. He hit a bump, and the rear door flew open . . ."

Tom went on as a chilling fog settled around the warm feeling in Sydney's chest. A curious sense of annoyance filtered into her consciousness, disturbing the contentment and kinship she'd felt moments earlier. Quite unnaturally, she wished Judy would go away.

She sighed. It wasn't Judy, she decided on second thought. It wasn't Judy's fault that she could talk so freely with Tom about his profession. It was her own fault that she couldn't be open and candid about it, that he hadn't told her any of his mortician jokes.

". . . he chases the coffin down the hill, through two sets of traffic lights, and through the front door of a pharmacy."

She sighed again. It would always be there, the gulf between his profession and her phobia. How long would they be able to live with their heads in the clouds, never talking about it, never sharing what one of them did with eight to ten hours of his day? Her heart tore painfully as she admitted the truth.

". . . he chased the coffin past the perfume

counter and the soda fountain to the back of the store, and then he saw the pharmacist and stopped. He was huffing and puffing and wheezing when he looked at the man and said, 'You got anything to stop this coffin?'"

Tom guffawed, and Judy groaned as Sydney's heart broke into a million unmendable pieces.

"No more," Judy insisted, hanging up the telephone with the force of her decision. "The next time that thing rings, you answer it. I won't tell him you're not here, when he knows as well as I do that you're sitting less than two feet away."

"I'm sorry," Sydney said, knowing the shame her friend felt at having to lie repeatedly whenever Tom called. Her own guilt was twofold. Not only was she being unfair and hurtful to Tom, she was embroiling her friend in a situation she should have taken care of days before.

"Dammit, Sydney," Tom'd said over the phone the day after their linguini dinner. "What the hell is going on here? So far you've come up with every flimsy excuse in the book not to see me again."

"It's not a flimsy excuse. I need time to think, and I can't think straight when you're around."

"That's the only time you *do* think straight," he argued. "When you're alone you get sidetracked from the real issues. You get confused and filled with doubt." He paused. "I want equal time."

"Equal time for what?"

"To convince you not to give up on us. That I'm right for you. To show you that we belong together."

Sydney was silent. She knew she should make a clean break, tell him it was over and be finished with it.

But how could she tell him that she wouldn't see him again, when her blundering heart was still enthralled with planning and building a life with Tom? Where were the words to convince him that what she thought to be the truth and what she wanted were one and the same? She knew she was hurting him, that she wasn't being fair, and that she was acting like a coward, but how could she tell him without choking on her own breath? Could she be absolutely certain she was making the right decision? Could she live with the finality of it? She couldn't. She knew she *should*, but she couldn't.

"I've never been so glad to see Monday in all my life," Judy continued to rant, more than a little angry with Sydney's behavior. "Now your receptionist'll have to lie for you all day and I can start looking at myself in the mirror again."

"I said I was sorry," she said, weakly. "I'll . . . I'll tell him. You won't have to lie to him anymore."

"When?"

"Today?"

"Today," Judy said firmly. And then, as a friend, she put her arm around Sydney's shoulder. "You've got a good heart, my friend. Listen to it," she said.

"It's in love. It's not listening to *me*." She laid her head on Judy's shoulder, hoping to tap into her calm logic. Hers was at an all-time low. "I feed it facts and tell it that Tom's not healthy for us, and it keeps saying, 'I love him.'"

Judy laughed. "Well, it appears to feel very strongly that it's right. Perhaps you should give its point of view some more consideration."

Sydney lifted her head and gave her a half smile. Judy was trying to be helpful, but it wasn't as simple as she kept trying to make it. Judy knew about her phobia; she knew about Tom's profession. As a rule, she was pretty quick to catch on to things, but at present she was lingering in her idealistic idea that love conquers all. Sydney knew better.

"You'd better get going, or you'll be late for work," she said, knowing that any further discussion about Tom would be useless.

"Look who's talking. You're not even dressed yet." Judy turned and looked back at Sydney from the door. "Maybe your heart knows something you haven't thought of yet."

"Like what? I've been over and through this so many times, I can't see straight anymore."

"So I've noticed," she said, and grinned. "And maybe that's the problem. Maybe your head's been so busy worrying, it hasn't had time to figure out what your heart already knows."

Sydney gave her a get-to-the-point stare.

"There's a lot of talk about love. People talk about it so much, it seems like a common, ordinary thing. But it isn't. It's very rare and very special. It's what every little girl dreams of . . . and what very few women find." She paused to choose her next words carefully. "Once your heart's known real love, it won't be content with anything less. And just because you found it once, that doesn't mean it'll be any easier to find a second time."

Sydney stared at the door long after Judy had closed it, and listened as her words resounded through the room like echoes in a cave. They were heart-words, from one woman to another, that rang true and clear and real.

Deep in thought, she entered the bathroom and let habit take over as she applied blush and mascara. Somewhere between brushing her teeth and leaving the bathroom to get dressed, a strange notion began to form in her mind.

It was not a whole thought, merely bits and pieces of an idea. But even the selection of her darkest clothing, a milk-chocolate brown skirt and jacket with a cream-colored silk blouse, was a deliberate step in the scheme forming in her head.

A glance at the clock told her she was going to be late for work, but she didn't quicken her pace. Work simply didn't fit into the plan she was hatching. She wouldn't be going to work that day.

Her life was upside down and needed to be set right. One minute she was dating safe, boring, predictable men, and on the heels of a wish for some variety in her life, all hell broke loose. A desire to meet a man she could tell her dreams to was all at once a man who shared her dreams and became an intrinsic part of them. A man who was neither boring nor predictable.

Her wishes had come true. She'd experienced the flip side to her sheltered, orderly lifestyle. She promised herself to be more careful the next time she made a wish.

But she'd also met the man she'd been looking for. A once-in-a-lifetime event—a phenomenon really, considering the number of people she knew who'd given up or settled for second best. And yet, a fear that she couldn't explain or control, a curse that shamed her, stood between them.

What did she believe, then? That fear was more powerful than love? That she was doomed to a drab, solitary existence because everything out of the ordinary threatened her sense of well-being? That she was so tightly wrapped in her own security blanket, she'd risk her heart and her future to stay that way? It didn't sound like her. She didn't recognize the coward she'd become.

Her tardiness helped her avoid the early morning bumper-to-bumper traffic, during which she usually did some of her best fretting. She soon discovered there was a strange correlation between motion on the freeway and the activity in her brain. The faster she drove, the quicker and less congested her thoughts were.

She'd never considered herself to be a quitter, a loser, or someone who was afraid to take a chance. She had accommodated her fear of dying all her life, but she'd never had to make a real sacrifice for it. Was she so afraid of dying that she wouldn't allow herself to live? And wasn't the line between living and existing drawn at the quality of one's life rather than its length?

"Damn right it is," she said aloud, bobbing her head to read the exit signs and steering the car into the far right-hand lane. "And I'm about to start living."

She took the first downtown exit she came to, her strategy formed solidly in her mind.

Sydney Isadora Wiesman was a fighter—not Rambo, mind you, but certainly someone to be reckoned with when it came to getting what she wanted. And she had her heart set on Tom Ghorman. Her fear was all that stood between her and the man she loved, and it was this same fear with which she was about to do battle. Once and for all time, she would stand up to the dread and terror that controlled her without cause or invitation. She was going face-to-face with her unseen enemy, and she had every intention of conquering it.

Well, she had every intention of conquering it while she parked her car in the lot outside the largest of the eight Ghorman mortuaries. And she had every intention of conquering her fears while she reapplied the lipstick she'd chewed off, and while she envisioned herself walking through the hallowed halls of the first Ghorman funeral home to the executive offices in the rear, where Tom would be waiting for her. The expression she pictured on Tom's face gave her the momentum to carry her to the front steps.

But there she faltered. The huge blond-brick building rose up before her like the gates of hell. Her heart pounded out an alarm, and adrenaline poured into her veins. She stood with one foot on the first step and watched the structure sway and lean heavily toward her. The thick wooden doors opened wide to expose the black abyss beyond, and her fingers went numb. The portal grew larger, wider, closer. Bile burned in the back of her throat.

"Oh, dear Lord," she muttered, frozen on the first step.

"It's all right, dear," a voice said. "Edward won't mind that you're a little late. Lord knows, the man took his own sweet time doing things when he was alive." There was a thoughtful pause. "*Alive* is certainly one word you could use to describe our Edward. What a pistol. Of course, *cad*, *cheat*, and *completely impossible* are just as descriptive. But he was a human being, and he deserves a certain amount of respect, don't you think?"

Sydney turned her head slowly until she could see the gray-haired middle-aged woman who'd spoken to her. She was tall and slim and had an air of elegance that one usually associated with affluence. She didn't, however, strike one spark of recognition in Sydney's distorted mind.

The woman smiled. "Oh, you had it bad, didn't you, dear?" she said kindly. She slipped an arm through Sydney's and began to walk with her up the steps. "You know, I've wondered about it a thousand times, and I have never been able to figure out what it was about Edward that got to us. He wasn't the richest man alive, and as far as his looks went . . . well, I have a poolman who Edward couldn't hold a candle to, even in his younger days."

Sydney couldn't believe her feet were moving. She told them not to. She told them to turn around and run back to the car, away from the darkness, away from the danger and the crazy woman beside her. But they ignored her. Step after step, they brought her closer and closer to the black void in which she would be lost forever if she crossed over its threshold.

She looked at the woman again and tried to protest, tried to make her understand the perils of getting too close to the eternal pit of doom that loomed before them, but her vocal cords were paralyzed.

The woman continued to speak in the absence of comment from Sydney. "He had that special something, though. I can't count the times that I made up my mind to be done with him, and then, out of the blue, there he was again. I wouldn't hear from him for months, and then suddenly he'd show up. No doubt he was the same with you. There are so many of us, one man couldn't possibly keep it up, so to speak, to satisfy us all."

What *was* she talking about? Sydney wondered. Her fear and the unfamiliar rambling of the woman were making her head swim.

"You're obviously one of the newer ones, so he probably saw you more often. He truly did prefer younger women, but he wasn't a love-'em-and-leave-'em type of man." She laughed. "We should form a sorority. We could call it We Bedded Eddy."

Okay. Enough was enough.

"What?" she asked the woman, frowning, confused beyond definition.

The woman looked at her and smiled knowingly. "I'm sorry. Ignore me." Sydney wished she could, but the woman had total control of her feet, and the yawning darkness was only steps away. "I don't handle this sort of thing very well, so I make jokes. I loved Edward, and I'm going to miss him. I'm just a little nervous to see what'll happen when we're all in the same room with his wife."

"Wife?" What *was* she talking about? Who was Edward? Who was "we"? And who cared about Edward's wife? She forced her feet to stop and steeled herself not to move another inch, but the woman was determined.

"Well, surely you must have realized she'd be here, dear," she said, opening the door and dragging Sydney inside with her.

"No," Sydney protested, fear gripping at her throat and abdomen. Gripping and twisting until she thought she might scream with the discomfort. Sydney shook her head. She was going blind. Except for the woman's face, she saw only nothingness.

"Truly," the woman said soothingly. "It'll be fine. I'll be right here beside you."

"No. I . . . can't see . . ." Her feet were moving again. Where was her will? Why couldn't she take control of her own body from this woman? she wondered, feeling hopelessly lost.

"It'll be fine. You'll see. You want to say good-bye to Edward, don't you?"

Although she couldn't see, her feet followed the woman. What little control she had left was instantly fried in the sensory overload.

She cried out and turned back to the door. Like the proverbial bat out of hell, she flew through the darkness using her own personal radar system to guide her.

"Please. Please. Let me out," she cried. "I have to get out of here."

"Ma'am? I'm Jeffrey—"

"I need to get out of here," she told him, straining her eyes to focus on his face. In her desperation her mind seized on another idea. "I need Tom. He knows. He'll get me out."

"Tom? Mr. Ghorman? Tom Ghorman?"

"Yes. Take me to his office. Please. I have to get out of here."

"He's not in his office. Perhaps there's something I can do for you. I'm the director of—"

"What do you mean he's not in his office? Didn't he come in to work today?"

"Well, yes, he did. But only to speak to the movers."

"What movers? What are you talking about? Can't anyone make sense in this place?" she wondered aloud, thinking it very possible that hell could be a place in which people spoke incongruously and illogically.

"Mr. Ghorman has had his offices moved to the Fargo Building on Hampton Avenue. But if there's anything I can do for you . . ."

"Why did he do that? I came all the way over here to show him how much I loved him and to see the expression on his face and to . . . and now . . ." She threw her hands out in despair. She wanted to cry, planned to cry as soon as she was safe.

"You could go over to the new office," he suggested, looping a comforting arm around her shoulders. "It's only fifteen minutes from here, and I'm sure he'd be glad to see you." He hesitated briefly. "You're the lady he met on TV, right?"

She nodded and took the bright white handkerchief he pressed between her fingers. She didn't need it yet, but it gave her something to do with her hands.

"Well, then, I know for sure that he'll be glad to see you. Tom and I are good friends."

She was walking again, but she had no idea where she was going. She could only hope that Tom's friend knew where he was going.

"Tell you what I'll do," he said encouragingly. "I'll call Tom and have him come back here. How's that?"

"But I can't stay here," she mumbled, twisting the handkerchief into a small rope. "I'm already blind, and I think I'm going to have a heart attack if I don't throw up first. I was so sure that I could do this. Just once. Just to show Tom that I love him."

"Well, I think he'll get the idea. If . . . if I seat you here, will you be all right for a second or two while I call Tom? You won't move, will you?" he asked, lowering her onto a deacon's bench in the foyer. She nodded. "Don't leave. I'll be right back."

She trembled in the darkness and listened to the hammering of her heart. Seconds ticked by sluggishly while her apprehensions multiplied. What if Jeffrey didn't come back? she agonized. What if she spent the few seconds she had left of her life sitting on a bench and didn't get to tell Tom that she loved him? Was this it? Was whatever lay beyond life a perpetual state of waiting? Like an eternal express lane? Was this all there was to dying? The blackness? The quiet? The waiting for something to happen? Was this all there was? She'd accomplished some of the major goals she'd set for her life, but there were still so many things she'd wanted to do. She wasn't finished living yet.

A door opened and closed far away, and she waited to hear Jeffery's voice again. She soon sensed a presence beside her and waited for him to speak.

Instead she heard someone weeping, softly, almost noiselessly, but with such deep pain and sorrow that it penetrated her terror and tore at the fiber of her heart.

Nature has a way of seeking out an equilibrium. All the elements in the universe eventually came into balance. Sydney was no exception. She knew agony when she heard it. And even through her own distress, she knew it was far greater than her own and instinctively sought a balance.

She turned her head and let the image of a young blond woman form in her consciousness. She was sitting next to her in a rigid upright position, eyes closed and damp with tears, her lower lip clenched tightly between her teeth as if the tension would control the quiver in her chin.

It was several long seconds before the woman picked up on Sydney's concern and sympathy and opened her eyes.

"I thought we had forever," the young woman muttered vaguely, stunned in her grief. "He promised me forever."

In the most natural, unthinking manner, Sydney reached out and gathered her into her arms. Without embarrassment and in no disgrace, the woman took comfort in her embrace. She cried tears from her soul. Bitter tears that sprang from the waste of a dream. Burning tears that came from the loss of a loved one. Biting tears that poured forth from the destruction of part of her spirit.

No words were exchanged. None were necessary. They were two women in pain, two women battling in defeat against the uncontrollable. Real and imaginary, the fear and torment were the same.

She held the young woman without weariness. There was a comfort in the sharing and understanding. There was a serenity in taking on a pain far more immediate than her own, and she couldn't help but wonder if Tom had ever felt the same sort of soul-linking kinship with his clients that she felt with the woman in her arms.

"Jeannie?" a soft voice broke in.

The head on Sydney's shoulder lifted at the sound of the voice. In a dazed fluster the woman looked at her.

"I'm sorry . . . I . . . Thank you. I'm very sorry," she said, her voice cracking with sudden awkwardness and discomfort.

"No. I'm sorry. For your loss."

She nodded, and her gaze met Sydney's with a unique type of silent gratitude. It was a look that Sydney would never forget.

A shadowy arm stretched out for the woman, and she left willingly, leaving Sydney alone on the deacon's bench. Still basking in the warm sensation of being human, Sydney sat back and took note of other shadows.

As if looking through darkly tinted sunglasses, she saw the few sparse pieces of finely carved antiques set about the vestibule. The Queen Anne chairs, the ornate pattern in the rug, the doors leading . . .

The doors!

Like a hostage with one final chance at escape, she didn't hesitate. She bolted for the main doors, already sucking in the fresh air of freedom when the doors opened.

"Sydney!"

"Tom!" It seemed fitting that he stood on the other side of the threshold in the sunlight, in her sanctuary, one step beyond the gloom.

"What are you doing here?" he asked, catching her in his arms as she flew past him.

She clung to him, safe at last. For long minutes they said nothing. It was enough to simply hold tight to each other, to feel loved, to belong. But the link between time and reality was a solid connection, and the truth couldn't be put off indefinitely.

"It didn't work, Tom," she said, disheartened and miserable, recognizing her opportunity to cry, to release her emotions. "I tried. I wanted it to work, but it didn't."

"What?" he asked, brushing short blond locks of hair away from her face and, when they were out of the way, brushing her cheek tenderly because he loved touching her. "What were you trying to do here?"

"Cure myself." She sniffed loudly. "I thought if I stood up to my fears, that I could find some way to deal with them, and we could—" she shrugged off the rest of her sentence, knowing it would hurt too much to list her hopeless wishes out loud.

"What happened?" he asked softly.

Through a blur of tears she met his gentle, inquisitive gaze and found it hard to sustain in her shame. She walked away from him as she spoke. "It was worse than I ever imagined. I was a basket case. Ask your friend Jeffrey." She sat down on the steps and wrapped her arms around her, gripping her jacket to contain the tremors that came in the aftershock. "I made a fool of myself, and of you."

"With who? Jeff?" he asked, sitting down beside her. "I don't think so. He told me you were beautiful and that I was a lucky guy."

"Everyone must go blind in there," she said, dejected.

Tom exhaled slowly, biding his time. He could see

that Sydney wasn't as happy with what she'd done as he was. She was upset and disappointed—he was thrilled. He concentrated on keeping a concerned frown on his face so he wouldn't grin, and waited for her to realize that he had her right where he wanted her.

"I don't know where I got the idea that this would work," she said, folding her arms across her knees and lowering her head to hide her tears. The gentling hand on her back did little to console her.

"If it matters at all, I'm not disappointed that it didn't work."

"It matters to me," she mumbled into her lap. "What if I never get over this fear I have of dying?"

"Then you never get over it."

"But what about us? You moved your office for me, didn't you?"

"Yes." He wanted to shout with joy. He wanted to kiss her, take her there and then on the steps of the mortuary and make love to her for the rest of time. He wanted to leap park benches and dance in a fountain. But it didn't seem like the right moment. "I moved the offices so that you could have as much or as little to do with my professional life as you could handle. But as far as I'm concerned, you don't have to have anything at all to do with it. You don't even have to think about it. Tell your friends I'm a mailman or an antiques dealer. Tell them anything you're comfortable with. It's my personal life I want you to be a part of, and I'm perfectly willing to keep them two complete and different entities."

"Why?" she cried, turning to look at him with a tearstained face, clearly lost to his thinking. "Why would you go to all that trouble for me? Why do you want me so badly, when you could have any number of normal women?"

His brows rose as if he were surprised by the question. "You mean aside from the fact that you're bright and intelligent and beautiful and kind and giving, why do I want you? I don't know. I guess I must love you," he said, looking more serious than he felt.

"You're as crazy as I am," she said. Her chin quivered, and she turned her head to keep him from seeing.

"I know. Isn't it great?"

"No! It isn't," she said, turning back to tell him why. His face was mere centimeters away, and his eyes were brimming with his emotions. Spring flowers bloomed in her heart under the steady scrutiny of his sky-blue eyes. If she were going to live forever—and she had every intention of doing so—she wanted to wake up every morning to blue skies and happiness, the kind she saw in his eyes.

"It is great," she murmured softly, touching his lower lip tentatively with a finger. "But it's not going to be easy."

"Name one good thing that is easy," he said before he kissed her.

"I do love you," she said.

"I know," he said before he kissed her again.

They sat shoulder to shoulder, heads together, fingers entwined, on the steps of the funeral home with no place special to go, no one more important to see, and nothing urgently needing their attention but their closeness.

"I'm proud of you," Tom said, his tone of voice telling her how much. "It took a lot of guts to come here for me."

Self-consciously she looked down at his long, well-shaped fingers and watched as they traced the lines on the palm of her hand. Braving her fears wasn't exactly the success she'd hoped for, but she conceded to the idea that it was a step in the right direction—Tom's direction. With all they had going for them, compromise in this part of their life together didn't seem like too much to ask. It beat the alternative.

"Did you . . . have you always worked in the office here, or have you done other things?" she asked, not sure if she really wanted to hear his answer.

"My father was running the show when I graduated from college. I . . . worked my way up the ladder. Why?"

"Were you ever the funeral director here?"

"Not here, but at the West Side home for a while."

"Did you ever hold someone when they were in pain? I mean, someone crying because of—" the flip of her hand finished her sentence.

"We call it comforting in the trade," he said, teasing her. Then more seriously he added, "And, yes, I've held someone in pain once or twice." He paused. "People are strange creatures. Most of them come here acting stoic and in control, and then go home and cry alone. It's sad really. Who besides a mortician or a doctor or maybe a minister would understand their grief better?" The long, hard look she gave him made him nervous. "Why do you ask?"

"You do good work, Tom Ghorman," she said, her voice quiet and inspired. "What you do is good."

"Well, thank you." He was grinning, but overall his expression was a little bewildered.

"I mean it. They—" she waved her hand in hesitation, "the dead people, don't have a lot to do with what goes on here, do they?"

As a rule, the deceased didn't do much of anything *anywhere*, but he thought he'd save this information for another time.

"No, they don't. There's a whole psychology that involves the death and dying process. If humans didn't love and feel pain and grief, there'd be nothing to it. We'd simply go on with our lives. And there'd be no fear of death. No sense of loss." He took an earnest grip on her fingers. "Fortunately, or unfortunately, we suffer a great deal with death. And recovery is a long, hard transition for most people. What we do is part of a . . . a ritual, a starting point. Like the opening ceremony at the Olympics. We help people to bury their dead, one of the first steps in the grieving process, which leads to starting over and beginning a new life."

"For those left behind," she said, more to herself than to him, yet he nodded. "The living."

If Tom knew half of the special feelings she'd experienced in the few moments she'd held the devastated young widow, it was no wonder that he had continued in the steps of his father, she pondered. Little boys didn't grow up dreaming of becoming morticians, and it couldn't have been high on the list of choices on career day in high school. That he had willfully picked dealing with grief-stricken individuals as a career spoke volumes to her about his innate goodness and sensitivity. She felt suddenly humbled in his presence.

"You're okay, Tom Ghorman . . . for a boy," she said, reminding him of the night they met.

"I'm glad you think so, because I don't intend to ask you again."

"Ask me what?"

"I've asked you three times to marry me, and three times you laughed in my face. It's your turn to ask me to marry you."

"Marry me?"

"Okay." He tightened his embrace and kissed her.

"That's not what I meant," she said, laughing, pushing him a nose distance away. "I thought the idea here was to give you more time to convince me that this can work and that you're the right man for me. Aren't we jumping the gun a little?"

"That was before I knew how much you loved me and how convinced you already were. The rest will take a little work and some compromising, but comparatively speaking, it should be child's play."

"You think so?" She wished she could be so sure.

"I know so."

"I'm trusting you, you know."

"I know," he murmured, his lips touching hers tenderly. He pulled her close and held her tight, vowing that she'd never regret loving him. He had a list as long as his arm of the things they could do to enable her to become comfortable with his profession. She might not ever embrace it or take an avid interest in it or show enthusiasm for it, but if the efforts she'd made already were any indication of her determination, she would eventually grow tolerant of it.

And the rest of their lives? Well, he pondered, they'd spent twelve hours together without once mentioning their occupations. So who was to say that twelve years wouldn't pass before they brought it up again? And twelve more after that? They had more to impart to each other than what they did to earn money. They had dreams to share and common interests to disclose and explore. They had a future to build. They had love and trust and support to give each other. They had laughter, understanding, and compassion to pass on to the other. As far as he was concerned, they had far more than they lacked in being unable to discuss his profession on a routine basis.

Sydney's thinking was much the same. If desire and determination had anything to do with one's destiny, hers and Tom's wasn't going to be too shabby, she decided. She was secure and content in his arms, but she wasn't fooling herself. Life with Tom wasn't going to be a cupcake for either of them. But it also wasn't going to be dull or boring or in any way a mere existence. It was going to be hard and real and full.

"Will you look at this?" Sydney heard someone say.

"Oh, dear," came another voice. "Is this the girl you were telling me about?"

She looked up over Tom's shoulder to see the crazy woman and a friend coming arm in arm down the steps.

"Really," the second woman snorted, showing obvious disapproval. "Do you think the steps of a funeral home is an appropriate place for this sort of thing? I'm sure Edward wouldn't approve."

"Now, now," the woman intervened, smiling kindly at Sydney. "This young woman is still deeply in love with Edward. She and I had a long talk about it earlier, didn't we, dear?" Sydney nodded once, not knowing why. Habit perhaps. Her body seemed accustomed to going along with the woman's every whim. "She'll always love Edward. There's no denying that."

"Who's Edward?" Tom asked, frowning.

"You don't understand," Sydney said finally. "Tom and I are in love. We're going to be married."

"For crying out loud," the friend cried out in horror. She looked from Sydney to Tom and said, "What nerve. To bring *him* here and flaunt him right under Edward's nose."

"Who's Edward?" Tom asked again, scowling deeply.

"Edward would approve of their falling in love, I'm sure," the first woman said. "Remember his motto: Take it when you can get it, especially if it's free." She hesitated, giving Tom a good long stare. "This young man reminds me a little of Edward. Doesn't he you, dear? Why, he has that same look in his eyes. You know, *that* look." The two older women exchanged knowing glances.

"*Who* is Edward?" Tom asked again from between clenched teeth.

"You still don't understand," Sydney said, smiling patiently at the ladies. She would have gone on to explain the whole situation had the crazy woman not turned back to her and with great benevolence tweaked her cheek.

"Don't you worry, dear. Edward's watching you, and he understands. He knows how much you love him," she said before she and her friend walked away.

"Who the hell is Edward?"

Eleven

"Welcome to *Electra-Love*," the recorded announcement began. "The game show where the whimsies of love meet the logic of technology, and where all the personal details of a first date are aired on nationwide television. Now, here's your host, Rex Swann!"

The applause sign flashed wildly, and the audience responded. Dapper Rex Swann all but bounced to center stage with his hands out in greeting.

"Thank you," he said. "Thank you and welcome. We have a special show planned for tonight in celebration of our tenth anniversary."

The crowd cheered, and he grinned his appreciation.

"Over the past ten years," he continued, "we've matched up over four thousand couples looking for an electra-love that would last a lifetime." He paused to let the crowd respond with enthusiasm. Then he laughed and said, "We've witnessed everything on this stage from marriage proposals to fistfights with jealous boyfriends. Some of our contestants have fallen in love, some have formed close friendships after their dates, and others have walked away disappointed. Every contestant, every couple, every date was different and unique, but they all had one thing in common. They were all looking for that one special someone they could share an electra-love with."

"This whole week, as part of our celebration, we're broadcasting our show live from the studio, and we've invited some of our success stories back, to see how those initial electrical sparks of love and romance have fared with time." A pregnant pause. "Some of you may remember this couple. . . ."

The studio monitors ran a seven-minute clip of a young couple whose date was recounted more as a comedy of errors than a romantic interlude, and the viewers clapped and cheered on cue when the couple agreed to give their audience matchup a second chance.

Rex Swann grinned in remembrance. "We'll take a short break and be back in two minutes with that same couple, four years after that *Electra-Love* date."

"Oh, dear Lord," Sydney muttered, closing her eyes as she sagged against a wall backstage. "I should have worn the pink dress. This one isn't hanging right, and it's white. I look like a huge fluffy cloud."

"Everything you wear hangs perfectly, and you know it," Tom said. "Otherwise you'd worry it to shreds. And I, personally, think you're the most beautiful fluffy cloud in the universe."

She gave him a nervous thanks-a-lot look, closed her eyes again, then said, "I can't believe we agreed to do this. The first time was like a nightmare."

"We had to, it was in the fine print. And the first time *was* a nightmare," Tom said with a smirk.

"You were being a royal pain in the ass, as I recall."

Her eyes snapped open. "Me?"

"You."

"Oh, sure. I tried to think things out logically and make a sane, rational decision, and *I* was the pain in the rear. But you ran around like a lovesick puppy, and you were . . . you were . . ." She frowned. "What were you?"

"I was the logical, sane, rational one pointing out the only possible decision you *could* make," he said, his blue eyes twinkling in that certain way that always made her knees a little weak.

She nodded, trying not to laugh. With her tongue in her cheek she said, "That's right. Silly me. I'd forgotten."

Sydney hadn't forgotten. She could call back nearly every second of the past four years. They were the best she'd ever known.

"It was later that you started acting really stupid," she said casually, as if she were recollecting the years in slow stages.

"Stupid? Me? When?" He couldn't believe his ears.

"You were late for our wedding."

"I had a flat on the freeway." He looked at her suspiciously. "You're never going to forgive me for that, are you?"

"Nope," she said, grinning. "I spent my wedding night with sand in my panties."

Tom groaned. "The hotel screwed up the reservations, not me." He smiled lasciviously. "And you didn't wear those panties for very long anyway."

She giggled, remembering that night on the beach fondly.

"What about the time you dropped me and then fell on me and broke my arm?" she reminded him.

"That shower we took was your idea, and the

soap made you slippery. A man only has so much control in a situation like that."

"Right. What about the time we went to sea?"

"Dropping anchor was your job."

"Yes, but you distracted me."

His face lit up. He reached out and tenderly caressed her cheek with the back of his fingers. "Yeah. It was great, huh?"

Their gazes met and held. They shared a single thought that shone in their eyes. Their love was great. She bit her bottom lip and nodded. "Until we went aground."

"You folks ready?" a young man in a large set of headphones asked, watching the stopwatch in his hand.

It was a different young man from the one Sydney remembered from her first ordeal on television, but she couldn't help wondering if they'd gone to the same school to learn how to be so blasé about everything.

"Oh, dear Lord," she muttered again, realizing that nothing short of a nationwide power outage was going to stop her from being on television again—live this time, with no taped safety net if she made a fool of herself.

Tom gave her a quick kiss.

"You're beautiful. Relax."

"I'm fat and my—"

"Ladies and gentlemen," they turned to the sound of Rex Swann's voice. "Let's welcome back Tom and Sydney Ghorman."

A wave of approval and good cheer rose up from the crowd as Tom pushed Sydney by the small of her back onto the stage. Dressed in a white maternity smock, she was eight and a half months pregnant, as big as a barn and hoping that no one would notice.

Tom had worn white slacks with his double-breasted captain's jacket to humor her. Their son, Trevor, was dressed in a white sailor suit. If she had to look like a ship, she couldn't have asked for a more handsome crew.

Pushing Shy Sydney and dragging the two-year-old, Trevor the Terrible, Tom managed a grin and to shake hands with their host as the three of them settled down on the loveseat across from Rex Swann.

"It's good to see you again," Rex said, his cordial appearance turning to a mask of utter surprise when Sydney suddenly stood up again and appeared to be leaving.

Tom glanced up at his wife and recognized the pained expression on her face. He sympathized with her. The loveseat was indeed an uncomfortable piece of furniture—and he wasn't pregnant. Calmly and without drawing too much attention, he gathered Trevor onto his lap and slid across the seat toward Rex Swann and the microphone, giving her plenty of space on which to set her wide girth before he gave her hand a gentle tug.

Sydney couldn't believe what was happening, didn't want to believe it. She sat down, refusing to think about it. They were picture perfect on the monitor, she thought, trying to divert her thoughts—good-looking, healthy, all dressed in white. They were the American dream family.

"Are you all comfy now?" Rex asked good-naturedly, eyeing Sydney as she sat bolt upright in the loveseat next to her husband and son.

Tom nodded and muttered something as he pried Trevor's fat little fingers from around the microphone.

"You two have been busy since your last visit," Rex commented with another glance at Sydney and a humorous smirk for the audience. "This is obviously your son."

Now holding both of Trevor's hands in his own, Tom smiled proudly at the dark-haired, blue-eyed boy and announced his son's name. He naturally glanced at his wife and was dismayed to see the uneasy frown on her face. He wished there was something he could do to make her more comfortable, but his smile of reassurance that their segment of the show wouldn't last long had to suffice.

"You know," Rex went on, "after your appearance here four years ago, the staff and I wouldn't have bet a plug nickel that the two of you would end up married." He paused. "Not to each other, anyway. How did that happen to come about?"

Tom looked to see if Sydney wanted to answer the question, but by the unmoving, glazed expression on her face, he assumed she didn't.

He shrugged. "Sydney finally saw the light and married me about six weeks after that show, Rex. We've been happy together ever since."

Sydney didn't look too happy when she leaned toward Tom and whispered, "Is that it? Are we finished? Can we go now?"

Rex and Tom looked at her in confusion and then exchanged baffled glances. The show had to go on.

"The, ah, the first year of marriage is an adjustment for anyone," Rex said, faltering, leery of Sydney's odd, stagestruck behavior. "Do you think yours was unusually difficult? Ah, I mean, considering the way things started out for the two of you?"

Sydney shifted her weight uncomfortably, and Tom's heart went out to her. He released one of Trevor's hands to take hers and give it a gentle squeeze. He winced with pain when she squeezed back, and at the same time realized that Rex was waiting for his answer.

"Ah, no," he said disjointedly, sending a perplexed glance at Sydney. "We had adjustments to make. Compromises, you know. We still don't have everything worked out, but we've come a long way."

There was an ear-piercing screech of electrical sound as Trevor grabbed the microphone off its support and accidentally dropped it on the floor. Rex was quick to right the mike while Tom wrestled with Trevor to keep him on his lap.

"Can we go now, honey?" Sydney whispered again. Tom stared at her with a vapid look of disbelief. She turned to Rex. "Isn't it time for a commercial?"

"You both had careers when you met," Rex stated hastily, reading the next question off the TelePrompTer, eager to have the segment finished before anything else went wrong. Turning the focus away from the flustered man and the squirming child, he addressed his next question to the weird and unwiedly woman. "Are you both still working at the jobs you had four years ago, Sydney?"

"No," she said flatly, and then apparently realizing that the camera was aimed straight at her, she simpered at him.

Over Trevor's head Tom saw the dumbfounded look on Rex's face and took pity on him.

"Actually, Rex," he said, looping his arms around Trevor like a pair of steel bands, "Sydney quit the job she had with the accounting firm and came to work for me." He grunted with effort, and Trevor cried out in frustration. "She handles all the accounting and taxes . . . all the stuff I don't have a head for." He chuckled. "Marrying a CPA turned out to be a pretty smart maneuver," he added, feeling that a little levity would also be a smart maneuver at that moment.

"So you live *and* work together?" Rex asked, clearly thinking Tom to be the crazier of the two adults before him.

"Well, no, not exactly." Trevor was trying to crawl down his back, so he turned the boy around and placed him firmly on his lap again. "We have separate offices on different floors of the same office building. In fact, we have two separate businesses, but I hired her accounting firm to handle all my paperwork. That way, she's involved with what I do . . . but then she isn't really. If that makes sense."

"Of course," Rex said, positively confused. "That makes for a . . . ah . . . a unique arrangement."

"Unique," Tom repeated, beginning to recognize a situation that they were sure to laugh about sometime in the distant future. "That's us all right."

"What kind of material is this?" Sydney asked distractedly, pinching the upholstery of the loveseat. "Did you Scotchguard it or does it have to be dry-cleaned?"

"As I recall, you liked to sail, Sydney," Rex said, reading the question in a loud, nervous voice. "Is that an activity the two of you enjoy sharing now?"

"Tom?" Sydney whispered, paying no heed to Rex's question, a note of urgency quivering in her voice. She gave her husband an apologetic smile as her eyes filled with tears, and then she groaned. "Oh, Tom."

"What?"

She leaned over and spoke softly into his ear.

"Okay," he said in an extremely calm voice that was inconsistent with the way he stood up suddenly and thrust Trevor into Rex Swann's arms. "It's okay, honey, we have plenty of time. Right? We have plenty of time?"

"Plenty of time for what?" Rex asked, watching Sydney shake her head while Trevor ripped the body mike off the lapel of his jacket. "What's happening?"

"She's in labor," Tom announced to the world, remembering what an ordeal Trevor's birth had been—an event that his wife could barely remember and that, much to his manly chagrin, had left her eager to repeat the experience almost immediately.

She made a noise that sounded very like a lonely coyote in the desert, and her body grew rigid as she fought the pain.

"It's all right, sweetheart. Try to relax. Take some deep breaths," he said, taking a few deep breaths of his own.

"Labor? Labor?" Rex questioned, as if he didn't know what the word meant . . . or perhaps couldn't believe that it was happening live on national television. "She's in labor?"

Sydney moaned loudly once again, and Rex Swann began to pray, "Oh, dear Lord."

THE EDITOR'S CORNER

As summer draws to a close, the nights get colder, and what better way could there be to warm up than by reading these fabulous LOVESWEPTs we have in store for you next month.

Joan Elliott Pickart leads the list with THE DEVIL IN STONE, LOVESWEPT #492, a powerful story of a love that flourishes despite difficult circumstances. When Robert Stone charges into Winter Holt's craft shop, he's a warrior on the warpath, out to expose a con artist. But he quickly realizes Winter is as honest as the day is long, and as beautiful as the desert sunrise. He longs to kiss away the sadness in her eyes, but she's vowed never to give her heart to another man—especially one who runs his life by a schedule and believes that love can be planned. It takes a lot of thrilling persuasion before Robert can convince Winter that their very different lives can be bridged. This is a romance to be cherished.

Humorous and emotional, playful and poignant, HEART OF DIXIE, LOVESWEPT #493, is another winner from Tami Hoag. Who can resist Jake Gannon, with his well-muscled body and blue eyes a girl can drown in? Dixie La Fontaine sure tries as she tows his overheated car to Mare's Nest, South Carolina. A perfect man like him would want a perfect woman, and that certainly isn't Dixie. But Jake knows a special lady when he sees one, and he's in hot pursuit of her down-home charm and all-delicious curves. If only he can share the secret of why he came to her town in the first place . . . A little mystery, a touch of Southern magic, and a lot of white-hot passion—who could ask for anything more?

A handsome devil of a rancher will send you swooning in THE LADY AND THE COWBOY, LOVESWEPT #494, by Charlotte Hughes. Dillon McKenzie is rugged, rowdy, and none too pleased that Abel Pratt's will divided his ranch equally between Dillon and a lady preacher! He doesn't want any goody-two-shoes telling him what to do, even one whose skin is silk and whose eyes light up the dark places in his heart. Rachael Caitland is determined to make the best of things, but the rough-and-tumble cowboy makes her yearn to risk caring for a man who's all wrong for her. Once Dillon tastes Rachael's fire, he'll move heaven and earth to make her break her rules. Give yourself a treat, and don't miss this compelling romance.

In SCANDALOUS, LOVESWEPT #495, Patricia Burroughs creates an unforgettable couple in the delectably brazen Paisley Vandermeir and the very respectable but oh so sexy Christopher Quincy Maitland. Born to a family constantly in the scandal sheets, Paisley is determined to commit one indiscretion and retire from notoriety. But when she throws herself at Chris, who belongs to another, she's shocked to find him a willing partner. Chris has a wild streak that's subdued by a comfortable engagement, but the intoxicating Paisley tempts him to break free. To claim her for his own, he'll brave trouble and reap its sweet reward. An utterly delightful book that will leave you smiling and looking for the next Patricia Burroughs LOVESWEPT.

Olivia Rupprecht pulls out all the stops in her next book, BEHIND CLOSED DOORS, LOVESWEPT #496, a potent love story that throbs with long-denied desire. When widower Myles Wellington learns that his sister-in-law, Faith, is carrying his child, he insists that she move into his house. Because she's loved him for so long and has been so alone, Faith has secretly agreed to help her sister with the gift of a child to Myles. How can she live with the one man who's forbidden to her, yet how can she resist grabbing at the chance to be with the only man whose touch sets her soul on fire? Myles wants this child, but he soon discovers he wants Faith even more. Together they struggle to break free of the past and exult in a passionate union. . . . Another fiery romance from Olivia.

Suzanne Forster concludes the month with a tale of smoldering sensuality, PRIVATE DANCER, LOVESWEPT #497. Sam Nichols is a tornado of sexual virility, and Bev Brewster has plenty of reservations about joining forces with him to hunt a con man on a cruise ship. Still, the job must be done, and Bev is professional enough to keep her distance from the deliciously dangerous Sam. But close quarters and steamy nights spark an inferno of ecstasy. Before long Sam's set her aflame with tantalizing caresses and thrilling kisses. But his dark anguish shadows the fierce pleasure they share. Once the chase is over and the criminal caught, will Sam's secret pain drive them apart forever?

Do remember to look for our FANFARE novels next month—four provocative and memorable stories with vastly different settings and times. First is GENUINE LIES by bestselling author Nora Roberts, a dazzling novel of Hollywood glamour, seductive secrets, and truth that can kill. MIRACLE by bestselling LOVESWEPT author Deborah Smith is an unforgettable story of love and the collision of worlds, from a shanty in the Georgia hills to a television studio in L.A. With warm, humorous, passionate characters, MIRACLE weaves a spell in which love may be improbable but never impossible. Award-winning author Susan Johnson joins the FANFARE list with her steamiest historical romance yet, FORBIDDEN. And don't miss bestselling LOVESWEPT author Judy Gill's BAD BILLY CULVER, a fabulous tale of sexual awakening, scandal, lies, and a passion that can't be denied.

We want to wish the best of luck to Carolyn Nichols, Publisher of LOVESWEPT. After nine eminently successful years, Carolyn has decided to leave publishing to embark on a new venture to help create jobs for the homeless. Carolyn joined Bantam Books in the spring of 1982 to create a line of contemporary romances. LOVESWEPT was launched to instant acclaim in May of 1983, and is now beloved by millions of fans worldwide. Numerous authors, now well-known and well-loved by loyal readers, have Carolyn to thank for daring to break the time-honored rules of romance writing, and for helping to usher in a vital new era of women's fiction.

For all of us here at LOVESWEPT, working with Carolyn has been an ever-stimulating experience. She has brought to her job a vitality and creativity that has spread throughout the staff and, we hope, will remain in the years to come. Carolyn is a consummate editor, a selfless, passionate, and unpretentious humanitarian, a loving mother, and our dear, dear friend. Though we will miss her deeply, we applaud her decision to turn her unmatchable drive toward helping those in need. We on the LOVESWEPT staff—Nita Taublib, Publishing Associate; Beth de Guzman, Editor; Susann Brailey, Consulting Editor; Elizabeth Barrett, Consulting Editor; and Tom Kleh, Assistant to the Publisher of Loveswept—vow to continue to bring you the best stories of consistently high quality that make each one a "keeper" in the best LOVESWEPT tradition.

Happy reading!

With every good wish,

Nita Taublib

Nita Taublib
Publishing Associate
LOVESWEPT/FANFARE
Bantam Books
New York, NY 10103

"Ms. Pickart has an unfailing ability to lighten the darkest day with her special blend of humor and romance." --*Romantic Times*

THE BONNIE BLUE

by Joan Elliott Pickart

Slade Ironbow was big, dark, and dangerous, a man any woman would want -- and the one rancher Becca Colten found impossible to resist!

Nobody could tame the rugged half-Apache with the devil's eyes, but when honor and a secret promise brought him to the Bonnie Blue ranch as her new foreman, Becca couldn't send him away. She needed his help to keep from losing her ranch to the man she suspected had murdered her father, but stubborn pride made her fight the mysterious loner whose body left her breathless and whose touch made her burn with needs she'd never understood.

THE SYMBOL OF GREAT WOMEN'S FICTION FROM BANTAM

On sale now at your local bookstore.

AN 291 - 7/91